"I WANT TO MAKE LOVE TO YOU."

Karen felt how strong Ariel's arms were around her, felt his long body pressed against her as he held her, saw the overpowering desire in his eyes.

She swallowed. "Then do it. Make love to me."

He slid his hand along her neck, over her shoulder, and down the tender skin inside her elbow where he lightly traced a circle that sent a tremor throughout her body. He lifted her arm to his lips and ran his tongue in the same sensitive place. Then Ariel pulled her to her feet and led her toward the bedroom. For a moment they stood face to face with barely any room between them. "And what makes this lady so happy?" he whispered.

"I want this," Karen said. "I really want this. . . ."

BARBARA BLACKTREE has been a dreamer all her life. Though her travel has been limited to the Northeast, she's "been to the moon and back" in her mind, where all dreams are romantic. Ms. Blacktree lives in upstate New York with her husband (tall, dark and handsome) and her son (short, blond and lovably pesky).

Dear Reader:

We at Rapture Romance hope you will continue to enjoy our four books each month as much as we enjoy bringing them to you. Our commitment remains strong to giving you only the best, by well-known favorite authors and exciting new writers.

We've used the comments and opinions we've heard from *you*, the reader, to make our selections, so please keep writing to us. Your letters have already helped us bring you better books—the kind you want— and we appreciate and depend on them. Of course, we are always happy to forward mail to our authors—writers need to hear from their fans!

Happy reading!

The Editors
Rapture Romance
New American Library
1633 Broadway
New York, NY 10019

ARIEL'S SONG

by
Barbara Blacktree

RAPTURE ROMANCE
NEW AMERICAN LIBRARY

PUBLISHER'S NOTE

This novel is a work of fiction. Names, characters, places, and incidents either are the product of the author's imagination or are used fictitiously, and any resemblance to actual persons, living or dead, events, or locales is entirely coincidental.

Copyright © 1984 by Barbara Coultry

SIGNET, SIGNET CLASSIC, MENTOR, PLUME, MERIDIAN AND NAL BOOKS
are published by New American Library,
1633 Broadway, New York, New York 10019

First Printing, January, 1985

1 2 3 4 5 6 7 8 9

PRINTED IN THE UNITED STATES OF AMERICA

To Dad and Lynn—
They should have been here.

Chapter One

"You can fill this prescription with any reputable optician," Karen said as she bent over the narrow desk. The prescription pad on which she wrote was new, only a single sheet had been torn from it and that one had been for her receptionist, Fran.

The attractively tanned young woman sat quietly watching from the examining chair until Karen had finished writing. "You know, Dr. Watts, I almost walked out of here when I saw you were a woman."

Karen looked up sharply from the slip of paper she'd been about to tear off the pad. "Don't tell me you have something against women."

"No . . . just female doctors." The patient smiled. "Until you proved me wrong, that is."

Karen had come up against this sentiment often enough in the past few years. She was almost immune to it now, although at first it had surprised her, since the procedures of ophthalmology had seemed so distant from the more intimate contact found with an internist or gynecologist. The surprise had turned into a belligerent resentment that she'd eventually tempered with acceptance and nurtured disregard. She could do nothing about what other people thought; all she could do was continue working with the highest degree of competency.

Yet her own practice sparkled in its newness and the young woman's remark had placed a smudge on Karen's first day. "How did I prove you wrong?" she asked.

"By knowing what you were doing. I guess I'm just not used to female doctors. What made you decide to be an eye doctor?"

Karen stared at the twenty-year-old woman who was now climbing down from the chair. "I've always liked eyes." It was true, she'd been fascinated by the shape, size, color, and abilities of eyes ever since she could remember. But that isn't all of it, she thought, not by a long shot.

When this last of only three patients for the day had paid her bill at the reception desk and left, Karen leaned across the high, narrow counter that separated the small office area from the waiting room. "Fran, you might as well go home, since there aren't any more patients today."

"Oh, but there's one more." Fran's contagious smile plumped out her already plump cheeks. She claimed it was the unavoidable, middle-aged spread, but Karen suspected it was more a lack of control when faced with beach plum preserves or fried fish, both of which were in natural abundance here on Cape Cod.

"Are you sure? I could have sworn there had been only three appointments made."

Fran switched the appointment book around so that Karen could see it and pointed a finger at the four-thirty slot. "He called while you were examining your three-o'clock patient. Didn't you hear the phone ring?"

Karen put up a hand to smooth her lustrous sable-brown hair. It needed no smoothing, caught up with pins as it was in a high swirl on top of her head. Greg had always liked her hair in this style. He'd said it gave her an air of sophisticated professionalism. Now, why was she remembering such things? She folded the thought neatly, tucked it away, and looked at the appointment book. "He couldn't make it any earlier? It's only three-thirty now."

"I got the impression he couldn't get away from work before then."

Even though Karen had come here to Falmouth to work, she still couldn't get rid of the misconception that everyone else in Cape Cod was on vacation. "What's his name?"

Fran lifted the book over the counter for Karen to take. "See for yourself."

Karen's sharply defined mouth curled up in amusement. "Ariel Singer? Did he mention whether his job entails carrying a harp and wearing flowing white robes with holes for the wings?"

Fran chuckled. "No, but that's close to the image I got, too."

Karen rested her large, smoke-colored eyes on Fran with affection. Why hadn't this sweet lady been her mother instead of . . . Well, that didn't really bear thinking about. Her own mother had always been good to her, hadn't she? But she'd always seemed nicer to Liza. Another thought to be refolded and stashed away. "Fran, why don't you go on home anyway? It's still an hour before the next appointment."

"But what about taking his history and typing it up?"

"I can take the history and you can type it up for the records tomorrow morning."

Fran gave Karen a speculative look. "Dr. Watts, if you'll excuse me for saying so, you're a beautiful woman and we don't know who this Ariel character is."

Beautiful? No one had ever called her beautiful. She'd always been taller than most of the other girls and it had given her a gangly self-image. As her body had filled out in all the right places, Karen had still felt as if she were all angles. Matching her body was her face, also composed of angles. Since when were angles on a woman beautiful? Even when Greg had claimed to be in love with her, he'd described her only as sophisticated-looking. Karen turned her vision outward again.

"I'm thirty years old, divorced, and have been known to be fully capable of scaring the wings off an angel with my acid tongue. I can take care of myself."

"But—"

"Besides," Karen interrupted, "anyone named Ariel Singer is certain to be short, skinny, and shy. Go on, Fran, I'll be fine."

Fran gave her employer a dubious glance before picking up her satchel-sized purse and coming out the half-door at the side of the small office. She crossed the waiting room, and as she opened the outside door, the salty ocean smell drifted in. It was mixed with a fishy odor that was good, not at all like the fish market Karen had known in Syracuse, New York.

Fran paused in the doorway. "I tried to get him to come in first thing tomorrow morning, but he insisted on today. Said he was concerned about a symptom he had."

"Don't worry about it, Fran. And if he's got an eye problem, he certainly won't be bothering to look at me as anything other than a doctor."

Fran's eyes swept over Karen's slender figure which was accentuated by a clinging blue silk dress. The fabric belied the discretion of its shirtwaist design and hinted that, beneath the folds, lay a gently curved body not unlike that of a gymnast. And like a gymnasts, the legs were long and slim.

Karen correctly interpreted the unspoken words in Fran's eyes. "Go on. As I said, I can take care of myself."

Karen watched the door close and then looked at her watch. Three-forty. Still fifty minutes to go before Ariel Singer arrived. She opened the door opposite the reception area and walked down the short hallway into her kitchen. She had enough time to fix cole slaw to go along with the potato salad and hot dogs she'd planned for her solitary dinner.

She smiled with satisfaction as she placed the small cabbage on the gleaming white counter. Her mother would have blanched at such mundane fare and Greg would have allowed it only for a picnic—something they'd never had before or during their marriage. It wasn't that he despised hot dogs and salads. It was just that they wouldn't have met with his high nutritional standards.

Karen sighed as she mixed mayonnaise into the shredded cabbage. She missed Greg. He'd been her friend and she'd loved him. But she'd never loved him as a woman does a man. They'd just fallen in together as interns at Upstate Medical Center in Syracuse, and their decision to open up a practice together had somehow brought on marriage.

They'd done well in their first year together—at least in their work, with Karen doing general ophthalmology and Greg specializing in surgery. But on the personal side, they'd failed. Karen looked back now on that bittersweet year. Greg had been easy to work with and fun to talk to. However, after her initiation into the sexual rites of marriage, she'd turned cold. None of it had come up to her expectations, and that had eventually colored the other areas of their marriage.

Prim. That's what Greg had finally called her, and she hadn't been able to disagree with him. Nor could she disagree with him when he suggested divorce. He'd insisted they could continue their practice together and Karen had thought they could too, but she hadn't wanted to. The divorce had set up the beginnings of a rebellion deep within her, a desire to fight back against all those things she should have warred with in her adolescence but hadn't because of fear of her distant father and strong-willed mother.

She'd written to her medical-school friend, Susan, who'd immediately invited Karen out to Boston to combine ophthalmology with otolaryngology. Susan had said that eyes went very well with her own ear, nose, and throat specialty, and Karen had agreed. Yet Karen had found Boston more congested than some of the noses her friend treated, and the high society she was expected to endure had reminded her too much of her own rigid childhood. Then she'd discovered Cape Cod, and with Greg's help in lieu of alimony, she'd set up her own practice in Falmouth.

Karen covered the bowl of cole slaw with plastic wrap, put it in the refrigerator, and then glanced at her watch. Four-fifteen. She'd better get back over to the office in case Mr. Singer arrived early.

Upon reentering the still-empty waiting room, she looked around. It had taken a full six months to complete the renovations and equipment installation, while it had taken her only three days to find and mortgage the house her office and living quarters were in. It had been amazingly perfect, almost as if it had waited on this quiet side street for Karen to discover.

The two rooms she'd made over for her practice had originally been a dining room and a back bedroom. It still left her the kitchen and living room downstairs and two enormous bedrooms upstairs with a bathroom large enough for all the necessities plus a sink enclosed in a counter running the full length of one wall.

Karen looked at the muted coral walls of the waiting room which were set off by the soft-brown chairs. A smile accentuated her high, angular cheekbones as she suddenly realized why she'd chosen these particular colors. Coral and brown had always complimented her dark complexion. So why did she decorate her waiting room instead of herself in these colors? She laughed in self-mockery. Maybe she should have placed a large hook on the wall where she could have hung herself opposite the door to greet her patients.

"It's a rare person who can laugh alone."

Karen snapped out of her silly reverie and turned to see a man standing in the open doorway. "It's a rare person who considers hanging herself on a wall like a picture." She hadn't meant to speak her thoughts, but it was a trait she'd never quite been able to squelch, even with strangers.

"You're a charming picture just as you are." His smile was slow, almost secretive.

Karen grabbed at her composure, but it leapt out of reach as she stared at the man framed in the doorway. Ariel Singer? He sported no halo, nor wings, but he was how a male angel should appear. She gauged the clearance between the top of the seven-foot door frame and his fairly long, wavy golden hair. He was tall, maybe six-three or -four. But it was his eyes more than his sun-kissed hair or his long, rangy body that held her suspended within the moment. They were the light blue of a hot summer sky, outlined in dark lashes that looked as if they were penned with India ink by an artist. A very good artist.

He stepped in and closed the door behind him. "I assume you're Dr. Watts and you may assume that I'm

Ariel Singer—if you're given to assumptions, that is."
He smiled at her with no upward curve to his mouth. It
was his almond-shaped eyes that smiled.

Karen felt oddly threatened. Had Fran been right?
Maybe she'd been too hasty in allowing her receptionist
to leave early. With an air of purpose, Karen walked
around and through the half-door into the small office.
"I let my receptionist go home a while ago." Now why
had she revealed the fact that she was alone? "I'll have
to take your history myself." She waved the clipboard
she'd picked up as if it were a shield.

He leaned across the narrow counter and Karen was
stunned, not by his eyes, but by the smell of him. Without thinking, she said, "Mr. Singer, you smell like the
deep blue sea!"

His laugh this time was with his mouth as well as his
eyes. "I ought to. I've been in it, on it, and around it all
day. Is it fish or foul?"

His pun made Karen join in with his laughter.
"Saltwater fish has its foulness pickled away by the
salt. It's not bad, I just didn't expect you to be carrying
the ocean in with you."

His full lips drew back together for a moment as he
stared at Karen. "I wouldn't have brought it with me if
I'd had the time to take a shower, but I was afraid to
miss this appointment. Think you can put up with a
merman for a while?"

Karen was more sure of standing his odor for an hour
than his amazing looks, but she remarked on neither
aspect and grabbed a pen instead. "Before I can exam-
ine you, I need certain information."

The short history she took told her only a little more
about Ariel Singer. He was thirty-one, a marine biologist, his home and work addresses were identical, for he
was a self-employed marine consultant. He had no

known allergies to anything other than, as he put it, unnatural perfumes worn by unnatural women, and he hadn't been on any medication for years, since he hadn't been sick in years.

Karen set the clipboard aside and came back out of the reception area. "Inner-sanctum time. By the way, what made you come to me instead of some other ophthalmologist?"

"You were recommended."

"Really? Hardly anyone knows me yet."

"My cousin does."

Karen cocked her head to the side, unaware of how the overhead light danced in her clear brown eyes. "Who's your cousin?"

"Susan Mathews."

Susan was her friend in Boston, the one with whom Karen had nearly combined practices. Karen smiled a little crookedly. "Small world, as they say."

He gazed down at her, accelerating her heartbeat with the look in his eyes. "Delightfully small."

While he arranged his long body into the examining chair and wasn't looking at her, Karen took the opportunity to fully gaze at him. He wore jeans faded to the same color as his eyes and she noted a frayed tear in the denim that covered his thigh. She could see some of his skin and she yanked her eyes away as an unfamiliar yearning crept over her.

His face was angular, with all the width at the top of his cheekbones, a width surely meant to accommodate his ethereal eyes. The deep tan of his skin only served to further accentuate the lightness of those eyes.

There was a small cleft in his chin that pointed back toward his full, sensuous mouth, a mouth that a woman would first want to touch with a delicate finger and then with her own lips.

His lips opened to show straight, white teeth. "Susan said you were an eye doctor, not a dentist."

Karen's eyes shot up to his. Thank goodness she wasn't given to blushing. She'd have glowed like a ruby at this moment. "Haven't you ever heard of eyeteeth?"

He smiled at her once again with just his eyes. "Yes, but my teeth are fine—it's an eye that's misbehaving."

"Which eye is it and what's it doing?"

"My left. It has two highly mobile spots. It started early this afternoon while I was using a microscope. Believe me, you don't want little black things in your eye while you're trying to see molecular structure."

Karen had an immediate suspicion of the cause of his problem, but she said nothing. A thorough exam, including a look right into the interior of those beautiful eyes, would be needed to confirm her suspicion.

The first part was easy. She had to be close to him, close enough to catch the man smell beneath the surface odor of the ocean, but not so close as to feel the heat of his skin. It was the second part that unnverved her and almost made her fall out of her doctor's role.

She sat back on her stool and reached for a small vial. "I'm going to put something into your eyes so I can see inside of them."

He glanced at the small vial. "Tropicamide?"

"How did you know?"

"I'm a repository for bits of information that are totally useless to me."

Karen smiled at him. There was something warm and compelling about him. Suddenly she wanted to know more than the brief, cold facts she'd written on the clipboard, but this wasn't the time. Right now, she was a doctor, not a woman.

She put drops into each of his eyes. "It'll be a little

while before the drug completes its dirty work. Have you ever had this done before?"

He wiped at his eyes with a tissue she'd handed him. "No, have you?"

Karen straightened her spine. "Of course. I needed to know what horrors I'd be committing on my patients."

"No need to get huffy, pretty lady." He grinned at her. "I wasn't attacking—just probing."

Pretty. There it was again. First Fran and now this man. She'd have to look at herself in a mirror later on. Under the guise of whiling away the time required for the drug to act, Karen asked, "What brought you to marine biology?"

"An old man of the sea."

Karen watched as his pupils began engulfing the rest of his eyes, like melting black onyx. The drug was working. "What do you mean?"

He looked beyond her as if seeing into another time. "When I was nine years old, I met a retired marine biologist. He filled the vacant hours of a lonely kid with friendship and mysterious answers to alien questions. I decided then that, when I grew up, I wanted to be a fish." He looked directly at her once again and chuckled. "I didn't realize I'd end up smelling like one too."

"It's not too bad. Do you spend your entire day in the ocean?"

"No. As a matter of fact, I spend more time in the lab or at the MBL library than in the water."

"MBL . . . Marine Biological Laboratory?"

"Right." He drew his straight-line brows together into a frown. "You said you wanted to look into my eyes. You said nothing about blinding me."

Karen leaned closer. His pupils were completely dilated. "Just a minute. I'll show you the source of your problem." She reached into a drawer, pulled out a small mirror, and handed it to him. "Look at your eyes."

Ariel looked into the mirror and then handed it back to her, "You're a sadist."

Karen smiled. "The drug wears off."

This was the part of the examination that unnerved her. She had to be close to him this time, close enough to feel his body heat, to feel his breath on her exposed neck. But as she peered into his eyes' interior, to the back where the optic nerve was visible, she forgot the man. She was lost in the world of retinas, capillaries, corneas, and yes, there it was, just what she'd suspected from the beginning.

Karen clicked off her small flashlight and slid away from him. "You have floaters."

"Whatever they are, they're as big as buoys."

Karen laughed. "Hardly." She took a plastic model of the eye from a shelf over the desk. "First, let me assure you that they're harmless, annoying but harmless." She opened the model and then explained in simple language about the vitreous humor and how, occasionally, a small portion solidifies and thus loses its transparency. Because the eye magnifies these tiny opacities, they appear much larger and more threatening than they really are.

"And I'll bet you're going to tell me there's no cure," he said.

"There isn't. Except for time. Next month or next year, you might suddenly realize your spots are gone. In the meantime, I'd suggest ignoring them as best you can."

Karen got up from her stool, indicating that the examination was complete. When Ariel Singer stood up, he towered over her.

"How much do I owe you for assaulting my person?"

His sense of humor appealed to her. It was sharp, like her own. "Twenty-five dollars for shooting lights into your eyes and fifteen for traumatizing your pupils."

He followed her back out into the waiting room, where sunlight streamed through two windows. He closed his eyes for a second. "I never thought I'd find sunshine less than beautiful. It hurts."

Karen looked at his eyes. His pupils were dilated so far that only a thin line of iris showed. "Do you have sunglasses?"

"No." He was bending over a checkbook he'd laid on the narrow counter of the office and had started to write in the date. Karen watched as he slowly formed each letter. There were only four letters to spell July but he could have written it ten times in the duration he'd taken for just the J.

He squinted at her. "I can't do it. I'm seeing double, even triple. I can manage my signature, but would you mind doing the rest?"

Karen filled in the remainder of the check, again noting the address as she had when he'd given it for the patient files—just a box number in a place called Centerville. She looked up and found herself missing the way his eyes had appeared before she'd drugged them.

"Where's Centerville?"

"A few miles this side of Hyannis."

Karen weighed the various possibilities, telling herself she shouldn't, that she knew nothing about this man other than that he was a scientist, that he had a prickly sense of humor, like she did, and that he was sensational looking like she wasn't. But she couldn't help herself.

"That's close to twenty miles from here. You're not planning on driving out there right now, are you?"

The large black spheres that were presently his eyes tried to focus on her with only small success. "How long does it take this devil's drug to wear off?"

Karen allowed the space of several heartbeats to slip past before she answered. "Four or five hours."

"Do you mind if I lurk on your doorstep until nine tonight?"

Would she have done this for another, less attractive man? "Yes, I do mind. I can't leave you as a miserable heap outside my door. I was about to close up the office, but if you'd like, you can come with me over to the living side of the house."

"I'd like that—as long as none of your windows face the setting sun."

Karen locked the waiting-room door and then led the way through the short hallway to her living room. It was a room she'd been proud of after she'd finished decorating it. The rug was plush, and depending on which way the nap lay, its color changed from wine to rust. She'd picked up these fluctuating hues in the cut-velvet couch and had accentuated the deep red in the two velvet chairs flanking the fireplace.

Glancing at the room, without turning back to her, he said, "Maybe I'd better try driving home."

Karen placed a hand on the back of the couch, digging her fingers into the soft texture. "Why? You'll have an accident."

"Because, if I sit on your furniture, it'll absorb my fishy essence."

"Then you can sit in the kitchen."

Following her into the kitchen, he sat down at the small round table in its center. Glancing at his eyes, Karen realized he wouldn't be capable of driving for another few hours.

"Look . . . it's not much, just hot dogs and a couple of

salads, but you're welcome to join me for dinner. I've already blinded you and I'd rather not add starvation to the list of my crimes against you." She hoped she was standing far enough away from him so that he couldn't see or sense the almost raw hope radiating from her.

He crossed an ankle over the thigh of his other leg and Karen noticed how the rip in his jeans tightened. She watched, tensely waiting for the fabric to tear and reveal more of his skin. But it didn't. She noticed too that he wore frayed sneakers with no socks. When she lifted her eyes back to his face, she discovered his temporarily onyx eyes firmly on her own. He was smiling, but only slightly.

"I have a better idea."

"Oh?"

"Can you drive a manual transmission?"

"Yes."

"Good. Then you can drive my car, your dinner, and me to my place where I can shower, change, and supply you with a great spot for a picnic."

The idea appealed to her, the man appealed to her, even the ripped jeans appealed to her. "I'd love it. I've never gone on a picnic."

"No? Then you had a deprived childhood and it's time to make up for it. You'd better change, though. Silk dresses and high heels can't withstand rocks, sand, and ocean winds."

Karen rummaged through the closet and bureau in her bedroom. Jeans, she'd need her jeans. She wished she'd worn them at least once before, but she hadn't had the opportunity. She'd bought them to replace the ones she'd discarded after painting and redecorating the house. Now, as she stood staring at herself in the full-length mirror on the inside of her bedroom door, she thought she looked nothing less than a city tourist in her stiff designer jeans and navy-blue tank top. Even her handmade leather sandals had never been worn.

When he opened the driver's side door for Karen, she slid into the bucket seat, moved it forward, and then stared at all the dials and the short stick shift.

"Why don't you go through the gears a few times while it's not running?" he asked, as he climbed in and closed the door.

Karen practiced a few times and found that it was easier than it looked. "What kind of car is this?"

"BMW 320i."

"It's interesting. It looks like a sedate little sedan on the outside, but like a hell-raiser inside."

He grinned crookedly. "If I were mean, I'd tell you it was just how it appears on the outside. But I'm not mean, so don't be fooled. It's a demon . . ."

Karen thought she heard him add ". . . like me," but she couldn't swear to it. What was she getting herself into? she wondered. However, as she drove out of Falmouth and onto the open road, the niggling worry disappeared. She'd never driven a sports car before.

She heard the man beside her chuckle, but was too engrossed in the way the car handled at breakneck speed around the curves in the road. She didn't question the exhilaration and sense of power she felt; she simply allowed it to take over.

His warm hand on her thigh brought her back down from her mental high and his words crash-landed her. "Fantasies are good, but in reality, they can kill."

Karen released the pressure of her foot on the accelerator. "Oh. I'm sorry. I just . . ."

"It's okay. It happens to lots of people the first time. It happened to me ten years ago. I survived, but the car didn't."

Karen glanced at the man beside her, the man whose

hand was thrilling her more than the car. "What happened?"

"I was twenty-one, with an overdeveloped sense of immortality, and I mistook the abilities of a brand-new Porsche." He looked at the road ahead, frowned at the bright summer light, and then looked back at Karen. "It never dawned on me that the car could only handle what I was capable of handling. The road turned suddenly and I didn't."

"Were you hurt?"

He grinned. "Want to see my scar?"

Karen slid her eyes sideways at him, realizing that his hand was still on her thigh. "Where is it?"

He removed his warm hand and started to unsnap his jeans.

"Wait a minute, Mr. Singer. That won't be necessary."

"Ariel. My name's Ariel. And you're right—it's an unnecessary scar in an unnecessary place."

Without looking at him, Karen could feel his smile. Would he really have removed his jeans? One part of her said yes, another said no.

He directed her off the main road, through Centerville and onto a smaller road. Then he told her to turn into a narrow road that was really more of a path. It ended next to a typical Cape Cod cottage.

"My castle, Dr. Watts."

"If I can call you Ariel, you can call me Karen."

Karen ascribed the odd look in his eyes to his still-enlarged pupils, but she wasn't quite as sure after he said, "Poof! Another psychotic fantasy blasted out of reach."

"You're disappointed in my name?" It was a common name, but certainly not ugly.

Ariel gave her that already familiar smile in which

only his eyes laughed. "It wouldn't have mattered whether your name was Veronica, Harriet, or Annabel Lee." He opened his door and said, "Come on. I want to get out of the sunlight and into the shower."

Karen decided that this man's mind drifted like wood on the sea, and with a mental shrug, she also climbed out of the car.

Ariel left her in the small living room while he disappeared into what Karen assumed was his bedroom, off which must have been the bath. She walked into the kitchen area which was set apart from the living room by a long counter on which she placed the basket Ariel had unceremoniously dropped just inside the door. She looked around the tiny kitchen and back into the living room. Everywhere she looked, she saw her favorite color combination, blue and green set off by the rich brown tones of wood.

She wandered back into the living room, where she could hear the shower's waterfall noise. There were no true chairs here. Instead, set on the royal-blue carpeting were three leaf-green beanbag chairs around a low, round table. No walls were visible as each available space was covered by bookshelves. Karen gravitated toward them, hoping to find some clue to the type of man with whom she'd haphazardly allowed herself to be alone.

She expected to find the books on oceanography, chemistry, and physics. She did not, however, expect the volumes of poetry, classical literature, and ancient history. And she felt herself coloring slightly at a small collection of what she considered only a hairbreadth away from pornography. She pulled out one of the books, heard the shower being turned off, and opened the oversized book, figuring he'd still have to get dried and dressed.

It was an astonishing collection of erotic Japanese prints, and in spite of telling herself she shouldn't, Karen looked at the page to which she'd opened. And then the flip side of the page. And the next.

"Find anything to suit your taste?"

Karen froze in embarrassment. She closed the book carefully and slipped it back into its accustomed place on the shelf. Shame combined with excitement and rippled through her as Ariel rested his hand on her shoulder. She could smell the faint soapy evidence of his clean body and she could feel the warmth of his closeness. She couldn't think of a thing to say; not even her usual sharp humor came to her rescue.

He pushed gently on her shoulder, bringing her around to face him. "Those are just fantasies, Karen. It's one of the ways we adults play. It's as harmless and as healthy as the child who shoots bad guys with a cap gun."

The compassion in Ariel's eyes brushed away a portion of her embarrassment. She felt drawn to that compassion and was suddenly surprised to find herself wondering if his lips would be as soft as his gaze.

"Would you like to find out?" His voice was a sensual whisper, but his grasp of her private thoughts startled her and she stepped backward.

Karen saw that he was only half-dressed in a clean pair of jeans. The tan skin of his torso was decorated with a few stray beads of moisture, and veins faintly traced the curves of his muscles. She breathed deeply, trying to shake the languor seeping through her, and forced herself to look up at Ariel.

"There's time enough for discovery. Why don't we have that picnic?"

"I wanted to wait just a little longer. I looked at

myself in the mirror and I think my poor eyes still prefer the shade."

Karen had to agree. His pupils had only just begun to contract. Yet she wanted desperately to get outside, where she felt that, somehow, the wind from the ocean would create space between them. She'd never been so violently attracted to a man, and though this in itself didn't frighten her, the knowledge that he would ultimately be disappointed in her—as she would be in herself—did frighten her.

Again, Ariel seemed to understand her fear, though she knew he couldn't possibly understand its source.

He stroked her cheek with a feather-light touch. "Let's while away the time with some of my treasures."

"You have treasure?" Her curiosity was immediately peaked.

"Of a sort. Nothing worth its weight in gold, but treasures to me." He walked over to a small case designed like a steel-banded coffer complete with an old-fashioned curved lid. He set it on the low round table, dragged one of the beanbag chairs over next to another one, and patted it. "Settle thy tension-ridden bones, lady, and I'll show ye me loot."

Karen eased herself into the squishy chair, finding it surprisingly comfortable. Ariel unlocked the chest with mock solemnity.

"I began filling this box when I was ten. Remember the retired marine biologist I mentioned who inspired my career?" Karen nodded. "Well, when I hadn't seen him on the beach for several weeks, I went to his house. His wife let me in and told me he'd died two weeks before. I remember feeling as if I'd lost the whole world. That man had been the only special thing in my life."

Karen watched as Ariel looked beyond her. She could see that he was once again viewing the lost landscape of a small child. She thought that if she looked into his eyes now with her special lights and instruments, she might see an elderly lady speaking to a sad little boy.

Ariel came back from his long-ago thoughts. "Anyway, his wife went into another room and then came back out holding this chest. She gave it to me along with the key and said her husband had placed a note inside of it several days before he'd died and he'd told her to give the chest to me as a parting gift."

Ariel reached in, took out a yellowed sheet of paper, and handed it to Karen.

She leaned foward to catch the light and read the words that had been written by a shaky hand: "Fill this box with treasure, yet be sure that it is a treasure of the heart. Pay no heed to what others hold precious, for you can never love precisely as another does. Lastly, show its contents only to those who you believe would also see the value of each item. It will tell you what words often cannot."

Karen reread the note to be sure she understood before returning it to Ariel. Leaning back once again in the chair, she asked, "Why are you showing this to me?"

As Ariel looked at her, she saw that his eyes were closer to normal. "Because I sense that if you'd been given such a box, you'd have filled it in a similar way."

"Is this a test?"

Ariel smiled at her and the smile gave her more discomfort than her own thoughts. "You don't need me to test you—I think you do that to yourself often enough without having me put you on trial. No"—he shook his head—"I only want to share a little of myself with you." He reached into the box, pulled out an object, and laid it in her hand. "My first treasure."

It was a shell, a very pretty one, but otherwise not

special. Karen turned it over several times. "Where is its significance?"

Ariel took it back and held it so that the small opening to its spiral interior was toward Karen. "On my way back home from the old marine biologist's house, I came across this shell at the very moment its tenant was vacating the premises. A hermit crab was abandoning his home because he'd grown too big for it. Even as a child, I realized that, somehow, that's what my friend had done when he'd died. The shell took away some of my sadness."

Karen pictured Ariel as a small boy and found herself wanting to reach out to smooth her hand over his blond head, to comfort him. She mentally shook off the notion. "You must have been a perceptive child."

Ariel reached into the box once again. "Possibly. But I believe all children are naturally born with a certain psychic understanding that's slowly buried beneath adult notions. Sometimes I think we grow down instead of up." He placed something in her hand.

The stone lying in her palm was a dusty-rose color, so smooth that she thought it must have been put to a jeweler's grinding wheel. Yet it was the shape that surprised her the most. "How could someone have carved a heart out of such a hard stone?"

"Some*one* didn't," Ariel said. "It was some*thing*—the ocean."

Karen inspected the stone more closely. "Did you find this too?"

"No, it was given to me when I was eighteen by a very special lady."

"A girlfriend?" Karen felt a sudden, peculiar sense of jealousy.

"Not exactly. She was more my teacher than anything." Karen relaxed slightly. "This lady had found the stone one day while we were walking along the beach. She gave it to me as a reminder of what she'd taught me."

"What was that?"

Ariel held her gaze and Karen realized that, even when serious, his eyes smiled. "There may very well come a time when I'll show you." He took the stone heart, put it back in the chest, locked the top, and then stood up offering a hand to help Karen out of the bean-bag chair.

"Let's have that picnic. My eyes feel better, but now my stomach is bothering me."

It was only a short walk from Ariel's cottage to the beach. Karen spread out an old blanket Ariel had provided while he walked along the shore in search of dry wood. He piled the sticks and twigs into a small hollow he'd dug in the sand, and while the fire's crackle combined musically with the swoosh-slap of the ocean's waves, he whittled the ends of two long sticks for roasting the hot dogs.

Finishing off her third hot dog, Karen squelched a burp. "I can't imagine what made me eat so much." Nor talk so much, she added to herself. She'd told him a great deal about her life, even touching on her marriage to Greg, though she'd carefully skirted the more private details.

"Salt-sea air does things to you." Ariel grinned at her. "Stay here. I'm going back up to the cottage for an antidote."

Karen watched his retreat, unable to take her eyes off the way his muscles moved in his back, like the alternately tightening and loosening of hemp rope. What was the matter with her? She felt so vulnerable with this man. What was so special about him? Oh, he was certainly handsome and he was intelligent, a quality she insisted on having in all her friends, but there was something else, something that she'd like to name. If she could name it, then maybe she could control the way it affected her.

She was staring out over the darkening ocean when she heard his feet brushing through the sand.

"I brought two antidotes. Put this one on for the chill that comes when the sun goes—which it's doing now."

Karen took the offered flannel shirt and slipped it on noticing that Ariel was already wearing another one. A pinpoint of disappointment poked through her as she realized his supple male body was now completely hidden. She subdued the thought. "And what's the other antidote?"

Ariel produced two small cordial glasses from his shirt pocket and handed them to her. "Hold these while I pour the medicine." From his other pocket he pulled a small sample bottle of green crème de menthe and shared its contents between the two glasses. "Calms the digestion and improves the spirit."

Karen was comfortable sitting next to Ariel as they drank the thick, mint liqueur and watched the world darken around them to the point where she suddenly realized she could no longer see the ocean. She could hear it fingering the beach and she could smell its salt on the stiffening breeze, but all she could see were lights twinkling farther down the shore in harbors and homes. She jumped a fraction when Ariel's voice broke the silence.

"Did you hear that?"

Karen listened. "What?" She wished she could see more of him in the darkness.

"Thunder."

With that, she saw a brief glow in the faraway sky over the ocean. "Is it coming this way?"

"It's headed right for us."

Karen shivered in the suddenly cooler, stronger breeze. "Maybe we'd better pack up and get out of its way."

She felt his arm slip around her shoulders and she allowed him to pull her close, assuring herself that it was only the warmth his body provided that she wanted.

Ariel slid his hand down her arm and back up to her shoulder. "Have you ever watched a storm blow in from the sea?"

"No."

"Then tonight you will."

Another flash of electricity stroked the sky, nearer this time. Ariel's voice was clear but muted by the distant thunder. "It's as if the elements were making love to each other. Imagine yourself the earth, a woman, and then the storm as a man."

The next burst of lightning illuminated Ariel's face long enough for Karen to see that he was staring at her. His face blended back into the night, and as the sky rumbled, he said, "The faraway lightning is the constriction of a lover's throat with the first glimmer of arousal. And the wind"—as if on cue, the breeze strengthened into a hard gust—"is the passion that blows unexpectedly through your mind."

A streak of lightning touched down to the ocean and Ariel's finger traced the sensitive skin from the inside of her elbows down to her wrist. "The first real touch of the lover."

Karen felt her heart accelerating at his brief touch, but more so at his words. Thunder rumbled louder than the waves, which were only now gaining violence from the storm moving in. Her heart seemed to pound right up into her head. She felt his warm breath in her ear.

"The thunder grows louder and comes faster. It's your heart speeding up with an expectancy shaped partly by need and partly by fear."

Much closer now, lightning streaked through the sky and the simultaneous explosion of thunder sent Karen mindlessly to Ariel's arms as he said, "The lover touches the earth and their bodies collide."

And Ariel's mouth was on hers, soft, with the underlying fierceness of the silken wolverine. She felt his tongue slide from one corner of her lips to the other while the first large raindrops splashed down on them. He probed with his tongue, slipping it with excruciating slowness into her own mouth, and it reminded her of a more intimate contact. Lightning turned her closed lids orange, a hot color to match her sudden overwhelming need. She lifted her hands, wanting to pull him down onto her, but they touched nothing. And her mouth touched nothing, for he'd drawn away from her. Only a leftover tingling remained on her lips and a stronger, less familiar sensation of yearning lingered in a more intimate place.

Ariel grabbed Karen's hand and pulled her to her feet. "This is fun, but I'd rather not be electrocuted before love. Afterward, I may accept it."

Snatching up the blanket and basket, they ran for the cottage, looking like apparitions illuminated by the natural strobes of lightning. By the time they were back inside Ariel's small living room, they were soaked, water streaming down their faces as if they'd just come out of the ocean.

Ariel put the basket on the floor and then straightened up to face Karen. One small lamp over the table in the kitchen lit the contours of the room and the angles of his face. "You have a choice. You can sit here in the living room with me while we try to make conversation, or you can come with me into my bed, where I'll dry the outside of your body with mine and moisten the inside the same way."

Ariel watched first pain, then shock, and finally anger break like successive waves across Karen's face. He felt her anger as a physical force, her words nearly drowning out his own silent ones.

Why are you yelling at me? What did I do? I just wanted to love you a little.

The image of a long-ago mother flared up, and for one moment in time, Karen and his mother merged and she was angry with him—or was it with all of life?—and she was going to leave him. Forever.

No, he thought. Remember the things Nicole taught you. Watch her. Watch this woman carefully and she'll reveal herself to you.

Ariel ignored Karen's ranting words; instead, he noticed how her hands were knotted in tension and fear, how her arms were crossed over her chest for protection.

Karen couldn't possibly be afraid of him specifically, he realized. Only when his own temper flared—and that was rare—could he be dangerous. It had to be something else. She had to be afraid of . . . Of what? Something he represented?

Ariel waited patiently until Karen paused for breath, and in that small space, he said as gently as he could, "I'll take you home."

Though she wasn't actually crouching by the passenger's door, it seemed that way as he drove slowly, thoughtfully back into Falmouth.

By the time he stopped the car in front of her house, he'd made his decision.

He'd held on to the fear of rejection for too many years. One after the other, he'd loved 'em and left 'em before they could leave him. It was about time he tempted his fates. Besides, Karen was special.

He looked over at her. In spite of the tension hardening her features, she was beautiful, but he wondered if she knew just how beautiful she was.

He had a feeling she didn't.

Chapter Two

Karen stared at the wipers' hypnotic motion and listened to their rhythmic thunking as they danced back and forth, back and forth, across the windshield of Ariel's car. She had wanted to follow him into his bedroom, possibly more than he had wanted it. What had stopped her? What had angered her so much that she'd lashed out at him with hard, almost vicious words? His eyes had revealed none of his thoughts, and when her raging monologue about men who suck pleasure from women had died down, he'd spoken quietly and simply. "I'll take you home."

The engine was still running, the wipers were still going about their business, but the car had stopped. Karen swam up from her tangled thoughts to see that they were in front of her house, its dark windows reflecting the emptiness within. She started to pull on the door handle when long fingers trapped her own. His left arm was in front of her, effectively barring her escape.

"I'm sorry." His voice was no more than a whisper.

"So am I," Karen said, but she was sure that her regrets were different from Ariel's.

"I'd like to see you again, but I'll be gone for the rest of the week." His breath touched her temple and cooled it where a single damp curl clung to her skin.

"Ariel, I don't think we're suited to each other." No? Then why was her heart still marching to the rhythm of the wipers?

Ariel was silent for a moment, but he didn't release her hand. "Did you know that all the oceans are really one? A molecule of water traveling from the North Atlantic down to the Antarctic, and back up to the North Pacific takes a thousand years."

Karen was nonplussed and looked into his face. "What on earth are you talking about?"

A smile flirted with his lips. "That molecule makes its journey in good faith that it'll reach its destination even though it goes through some of the coldest waters before it rediscovers the warmth it seeks."

Now she knew what he meant. She stared at the water streaking down the window. "I doubt you'll find any warmth here."

His sigh underscored the closed-in sensation of sitting in a car washed by rain. "Karen . . . let's start over again. Please?"

She was afraid to look at him, afraid she might discover duplicity in his beautiful eyes, but the fear couldn't hold her back from glancing over at him. Just in case she never saw Ariel again, she wanted to remember every detail—his full mouth, his smooth skin, his high cheekbones, his golden hair, and most of all, his blue, almond-shaped eyes, which were so full of laughter.

But his eyes weren't laughing when she looked into them. They were serious and they held all the sincerity she'd feared would be absent.

"Yes," she said quietly, "let's do that. Let's start over again."

"Invite me in for coffee."

"Would you like to come in for coffee?"

A smile once again sparkled from his eyes. "I don't know. It's kind of late and I have to get up early tomorrow."

Karen felt an urge to slap his handsome face, but the moment passed and she relaxed with a smile. "You don't behave very well."

"It's your fault." His grin dissolved. "The truth is that you've gotten me completely rattled."

Yes, she'd probably rattled his ego. With looks and charm such as he had, he was no doubt used to having women fall all over him. Well, she'd give him coffee but nothing else.

Karen dug her keys from the bottom of her purse while Ariel turned off the car and grabbed the picnic basket. Minutes later, thoroughly wet from the downpour, they walked into her kitchen.

Handing him a clean towel and taking one for herself, she concentrated on drying her hair and then fixing the coffee, all the while puzzling over how to start again.

She turned away from the coffee maker, having explored each meager idea in vain, to find Ariel's eyes shaped into the already familiar smile. It was a beatific expression, as if he'd just won a secret victory; it worried her.

"Ariel, I really haven't the least notion of how to start over again." She looked at his long legs spreading out from where he sat sideways at the table, and suddenly she was laughing. "I'll bet you get tripped over a lot."

He looked down at his legs and then grinned up at her. "Ever since I was sixteen, someone has been yelling at me to put my legs under the table. Only thing is, when I put them under the table, they yelled at me to stop stretching my legs out to the other side. And that's a very good beginning."

"What is?"

"You said you didn't know how to start over again." He looked toward the sputtering coffee maker. "Do you always make real coffee?"

Karen sat down across the table from Ariel, not wanting to see his legs, not wanting the thoughts they inspired of sheets tangling in the night. "I hate instant coffee."

"Me too, but it's fast and easy at five in the morning."

Karen cringed at the thought of five A.M. "Why do you get up so early?"

"The Ariel bird catches the sea worm." He ignored her laughter and stood up, taking a formal bow. "Let me introduce myself. I'm Ariel Singer, graduate of MIT with a bachelor's degree in biology and a master's in both chemistry and oceanography. I'm also a graduate of Woods Hole Oceanographic Institution with a Ph.D. in marine biology. I worked for three years at the institution until I realized I was spending all my time studying only what might bring me research grants. That's when I whistled a good-bye tune and struck out on my own. I'm now Dr. Ariel Singer, marine-biology consultant, taker of high-paying jobs that entail diving among polluted seaweed, shooting pictures of barracuda who take bets with each other on how long it'll take to make me disappear, and staring at pinheads of ocean water through a microscope." He sat back down. "And there you have it."

His light, friendly attitude spread into Karen, and throwing away her reluctance to bring those long legs back into view, she stood up, checked the coffee, then turned to see Ariel's eyes broadcasting a combination of humor and curiosity.

"And I'm Karen Watts, Doctor of Ophthalmology. Like you, I have degrees in both biology and chemistry but my Ph.D. is in medicine. I graduated from Syracuse University and then did my postgraduate work at Upstate Medical Center. I combined practices and lives with another ophthalmologist for a while, but again like you, I left what seemed a prison and struck out on my own here in Falmouth." She paused and heard no more gurgles from the machine at her back. "And the coffee's done."

His silence was eerie. Her fingers quivered as she poured out two cups of coffee and set out sugar and milk. What was he thinking?

"I never said the institution was a prison, just that it wasn't what I wanted."

Karen watched the steam curling up from her coffee. Of all that she'd said, he had to latch on to that one word: "prison." She'd have to explain it while only half-understanding it herself.

"I guess what I meant by prison was that I wasn't doing what I really wanted to do."

"Why?"

What business was it of his? Karen looked up to see real interest glowing in his eyes and she suddenly wanted to tell this man something. But she couldn't figure out what that something was.

"I'm not sure." She groped through memories and said the first thing to come to mind. "He didn't like hot dogs and I didn't like intellectual discussions at three A.M.."

Ariel chuckled as he reached for the sugar. "Obviously a severe case of incompatibility."

"You think divorce is funny?"

"No," he said, ladling two spoonfuls into his cup. "I think you probably just put into a single sentence what it takes most people several hours to explain. It was a pleasure to hear it."

Mollified, Karen watched Ariel stir in the excessive sugar and then enough milk to turn his coffee a light beige. "For heaven's sake, how can you drink it like that?"

Ariel looked at her, then down at his cup, his eyebrows drawn into a perplexed line. "It tastes good. Besides, I've fixed coffee like this since I was twelve when I was given permission to drink it." He laughed. "I think they let me drink it hoping it would stunt my growth."

"Obviously, Dr. Singer, the ploy didn't work. But really, that's the way children drink coffee, not grown men."

"Then I guess I'm not a grown man."

Karen scanned the visible top half of him. He certainly *looked* like a grown man, maybe even a touch overgrown. Yet there was truth in his simple statement. In some way, Ariel was as artless and as unaffected as a child. Yes, he was the sort of man who'd never drink his coffee black even if other people felt it was the masculine thing to do.

A smile toyed about her mouth. "I'll bet you like jelly beans too."

"All but the black ones. Same with Necco Wafers."

He was laughing and then she too was laughing. She liked this man who drank milky, sweet coffee and who liked jelly beans and Necco wafers—all but the black ones. She liked this man whose legs were something to trip over and whose eyes seemed filled with expansive joy in just the simple act of living.

Karen took a sip of her coffee and then realized something that wasn't very important but that struck her with its symbolism. She *hated* black coffee. How many years had she been doing things only to live up to the image other people expected of her?

Ariel watched as she added a spoonful of sugar and a large dose of milk to her cup. "I'm a bad influence."

She couldn't control a sheepish smile. "No. You're a good influence. It's about time I realized that black coffee and severe hairstyles are only what *other* people see as sophistication. It's something you appear to have learned a long time ago."

"Karen," he said quietly, seriously, "I've never been sophisticated. I've tried at times but failed miserably. Something inside of me keeps saying I can't be urbane and still be happy."

She looked at him intently for the first time since they'd left his cottage. How perfect he seemed with his heart-stopping face and body, his natural grace of mind, and his strong intellect.

No, not perfect. No one was perfect. He'd made a mistake back at his cottage by pushing her too hard and too fast. But she'd made a mistake too.

"Ariel, back at your place, I . . . overreacted. I could have handled it with more"—she laughed in self-derision—"with more sophistication." His lack of response irked her. "And you could have been more of a gentleman and not expected so much so soon."

Without expression, he asked, "When is it a gentlemanly time to start expecting?"

Anger replaced peevishness. "I prefer getting to know a person better."

"Well, you know me better."

"Yes, but . . ." She didn't know what she'd been about to say because she was watching with deep suspicion as Ariel stood up and walked around the table to tower over her.

"You know I'm a marine biologist. You know I'm

smart enough to get a doctorate from an institution that offers few people the opportunity. You know that I'm honest. You're aware that our interests are basically similar. You know I'm attracted to both your mind and your body." His almond eyes narrowed. "And, dammit, you're just as attracted to me, so what the hell's wrong with my wanting to make love to you?"

Nothing. "Everything!" She stood up, trying to take away his advantage of height. "You list off your attributes as if you're sure that that's all you need. Ariel has brains. Ariel has a doctorate. Ariel is attractive. Therefore, Karen should reward Ariel for being so good by going to bed with him."

"We could use the floor instead."

Karen's hand rose with the furious need to slap his laughing mouth, but in one swift movement he wrapped his arms around her, pinning her arms to her sides before bending his head down to hers.

She wanted to struggle against his kiss, to hold on to her anger, but his mouth was so soft and hot and his tongue slipping between her too-pliant lips was so gentle and intimate that she responded shamelessly.

Ariel withdrew a fraction. "You want that reward as much as I do."

He was right, she knew he was right, but his confidence in his own success, his astonishingly brazen attitude, felt like a sledgehammer trying to beat down her carefully built wall. Karen had never known a man like this. He scared her, but her response to him and the inevitable pain it would bring scared her more. She knew she couldn't satisfy a man such as Ariel.

Karen twisted out of his arms and turned her back on him. "Go away. Go away and leave me alone."

"I'll go away"—his footsteps were quiet as he walked out of the kitchen—"but I won't leave you alone."

Then he was gone, slamming the door behind him.

Karen turned slowly, swallowing down tears of regret. The first item she focused on was a very light-colored, half-finished cup of sweet liquid.

The first twenty-four hours after Karen had met Ariel seemed like a lifetime. When the telephone rang, she snatched it up in midring, hoping it was he.

"Is that you Karen?" It was Susan.

"No, it's the ghost of Christmas Past vacationing by the sea."

"Well, Ms. Ghost," Susan replied with a laugh, "would you accept a haunting from the ghost of Christmas Present at your gloomy mansion in the near future? Friday to be precise?"

"On one condition," Karen answered.

"That I don't rattle my chains at three A.M.?"

"No, that you stay for the whole weekend." It would be good to have company, particularly that of her closest friend.

"It's a deal." Susan paused. "Uh, would it bother you if I told you I'd be gone from Saturday afternoon until maybe late Saturday night?"

"Only if you refuse to tell me why."

Susan heaved an exaggerated sigh of relief. "I promise that, if you ever need it, I'll be more than glad to return the favor. The reason I'll be gone is that Jordan just called and wants me to spend the day and evening with him."

Jordan? The name seemed familair, but Karen couldn't find its proper mental cubbyhole. "Who's he?"

"Don't you remember all those stories I used to tell you about Ari's friend Jordan and the mischief they'd get into?"

"Oh, yeah. Isn't that the guy your mother wouldn't

let into her house for a month after he stocked the swimming pool with trout or something?'"

Susan's sudden laugh came out as a snort. "That's the one. The fish incident eventually blew over and Mom let me go out with him again as long as we doubled with Ari and whomever. Of course, it never dawned on Mom that Ari was really just as bad as Jordan. Ari was simply quieter about it."

Karen smiled as she remembered the various "incidents" Susan had related to her over the course of the years they'd spent together in college and then during their internships at Upstate Medical Center. "It's funny, even though I've never met Ari, I feel like I know your brother after all the stories you've told me."

"Uh . . . Karen?"

"What?" Karen heard an unfamiliar strain in Susan's voice.

"Ari's not really my brother."

Karen couldn't respond. Why had her best friend been lying to her for years?

Susan cleared her throat. "He's my cousin." When Karen still said nothing, Susan rushed on. "I know it's silly, but it's all because I had what every child in the world ought to have. I had two parents who loved me—I mean really *loved* me—I had everything material I could ever want. This is awful. I mean it's just plain dumb, but instead of being happy and grateful and whatever else I should have been, I wanted a lot more . . . or a lot less."

"You're right," Karen said, a smile in her voice. "This is dumb."

"You grew up with a lot of love and affluence yourself." Susan's words sounded accusatory until, after a short pause, she added, "Didn't it make you feel different from the other kids?"

"It's hard to say, Susan. I *was* different. My mother was always assuring me of just how different I really was. But I've told you about how I was the genius while my sister, Liza, was the beauty of the family. Remember?"

"Yes. Anyway, there I was, this little rich kid with absurdly wonderful parents. Not a trouble in the world, and in some childish way I felt I was sorely lacking. I was leading a life that was so good as to be positively monotonous, and I felt like a big fat zero of a kid. Then Ari came along and added some honest-to-goodness drama to my life. Unfortunately, I was too young for it to dawn on me that what I saw as drama, Ari saw as pure misery."

"This is," Karen said "utterly confusing. You've always described Ari as being surrounded by laughter."

"I know. And he was. Is. But you see, technically he was an orphan, and to wee Susy Mathews, who'd always thought she was boring and that it was because her life was so easy, the idea of being a lonely, troubled orphan . . . Well, the whole idea sparkled with romance. Little Orphan Ari—you know?"

Karen laughed. "That still doesn't explain why you told me he was your brother when he was actually your cous—" Good God! How stupid could one person be? But Susan was talking again and Karen's next question had to wait.

"Oh, Karen, it was just that you were so smart and beautiful. And don't raise your perfect eyebrows at me. You *are* beautiful. On top of it all." Susan giggled nervously. "On top of it all, you obviously had a neurotic mother, which made you much less boring than I was. So I told you Ari was my brother. I felt more melodramatic that way."

Karen decided she'd digest all this later when she was alone. At the moment, there was something far more pressing. "Susan?"

"Yes?"

"What's Ari's full name?"

"Ariel Singer. Gee, I guess he hasn't made an appointment with you yet. He called me the other day about spots or something in his eye and I told him—"

"I met him."

"What?"

"I said I met him. It never occurred to me he was Ari. He called you his cousin."

"I'm sorry, Karen. The only good defense I have is that he and I have lived like brother and sister for years."

"You don't have to apologize. No harm done." Except for one thing, Karen thought. Now she couldn't tell Susan how he made her feel. Her friend was too close to him.

Karen unconsciously coiled the telephone wire around her forefinger, then uncoiled it. "You know something, Susan?"

"What?"

"You haven't got a boring bone in your body." Pause. "And I'm not beautiful."

After hanging up, Karen stood staring at the phone, wondering why she was so rattled by the discovery that Ari and Ariel were the same man. It couldn't really change anything, could it?

On Thursday night, after two complete days of hiding the answer from herself, it slipped out while she was sauntering through other areas of her mind. She'd been paging through her college yearbook, enjoying the trip back into a time of innocent hope and determination. She looked at the small photo of Susan with her medium brown, flyaway curls that framed a cherubic face. Medium also were her nose, her skin tone, and her brown eyes. The only thing about Susan that wasn't medium was her mouth. It was full and soft and blatantly sensual.

That was it. Karen could still picture Susan's mouth forming the words she'd said years ago in their dormitory room.

"My brother's a honeybee when it comes to women. He flits from flower to flower, collecting all the nectar he can. Once he's sucked out all the sweet stuff, he flies away."

Ariel was the brother Susan had been describing. A womanizer. A man who couldn't possibly provide what Karen so desperately needed at this point in her life: a reaffirmation of her femininity. Karen slammed the book shut.

Friday was an easy day in which to forget her disturbing thoughts. Apparently, Ariel had recommended her to a few of his fellow scientists who, in turn, were recommending her to still others. She'd had a full schedule all day, and now, walking from the office into her living room, her satisfaction was increased by the anticipation of having Susan visit for the weekend.

Two knocks sounded on the door and Susan walked in. "The ghost has arrived!"

Karen hugged her best friend. "Are ghosts supposed to get hungry?"

"A ghost after my own heart." Susan tugged on Karen's arm. "Come on. Let's go to some touristy clam shack where we can gorge ourselves, belch discreetly, and yak up a storm worthy of an ocean."

Not long after, Karen and Susan sat consuming great quantities of fried clams on the patio deck of a restaurant that overlooked Falmouth Harbor. It had been a day filled with the brilliance of sun-sparkled waters and the faded sky of midsummer heat. Neither woman wanted to miss the sunset, and so they'd chosen to sit on the deck rather than inside the restaurant.

Susan sat back and groaned as if in pain. "I wish I were as tall as you."

"Why? You're fine just the way you are."

Susan grinned. "That's my usual opinion, but when I get to eating fried clams, I always wish my body were longer so that it could accommodate more of these little fried beasties."

Susan's manner of talking never seemed to put her very high intellect on display, a characteristic that had once annoyed Karen but that now put her at ease. "Susan, how come your Phi Beta Kappa key never shows?"

"It shows when I need it. I sure as hell don't need it while I'm pigging out on clams. I mean, how can I hold a decent conversation concerning the various theories of evolution while trying to surreptitiously dig a clam out of my left rear molar?"

Karen laughed. "I suppose you're right. Can you work on that wedged clam and, at the same time, fill me in on all this Jordan business? You used to talk a lot about Jordan, but you never mentioned dating him before our phone conversation the other night."

Susan sighed. "I suppose I never mentioned it because what we did was never what you could call actual dating. Usually, it was just him and Ari and me going out to raise a little hell whenever Ari brought him home for a weekend. When Ari took a date along, I'd pretend that Jordan was my date. But he wasn't really. We were just sort of hanging out together. And sometimes, I didn't go along at all because Jordan would have a real date that night."

Karen could see the wistfulness in Susan's eyes and her heart went out to her friend. "Didn't you *ever* go out on an honest-to-goodness date with him?"

"This will be the first time."

The sky was turning a buttercup yellow over the more distant Buzzards Bay and Karen stared at the happy color, aware that it was but a fleeting thing. She looked back at Susan. "Tell me about him, not the shenanigans of him and Ariel, but about Jordan. Who is he and what's he like?"

Susan stared for a moment at the yellow sky before beginning to speak. "Jordan Hasan. Arab by heritage but born in Nebraska. His parents named him after the country they were originally from. According to Jordan, his parents got married in spite of parental protest on both sides because of their differing backgrounds. I'm sure you know that Jordan is a land that's been immersed in political and religious conflict for years. Well, his mother was on one side of the conflict while his father was on the other. But they loved each other and got married anyway. It didn't take them long to realize that, in a way, their parents had been right. They found themselves arguing more and more because of their opposing viewpoints. Finally, they decided that if they were to preserve their love, they'd have to leave the country that supported their differences. So they emigrated to the States, somehow landed in Nebraska, and raised a family of five children. Jordan was the middle child and he claims that it's that particular position in the family that's at the base of his personality. His parents were too busy pushing the older children toward achievement and coddling the younger ones to pay much attention to what he was up to at any given moment. He never seems to admit to the fact that he's been a pretty high achiever on his own."

"How's that?" Karen prompted.

"Somehow, this Arab from Nebraska developed a love for the sea and found his way to MIT at the same time Ari did. They got their bachelor-of-science degrees at the same time, and according to Ariel, the only reason Jordan didn't reach the top of the class was because he was always more literally immersed in the ocean than he was in the study of it. Ari's a fish—Jordan's a submarine."

Karen laughed at the description. "For some reason, I was sure they were both human males."

"Occasionally, I'm not so sure. Maybe someday you'll get to see my dear cousin when he's swimming. He turns from a man into some mythical fish like a merman. It's hypnotic to watch him. And Jordan swims well too, but his true love is scuba diving. I think that's why he chose marine archaeology as a profession. Like Ariel, Jordan has a doctorate."

"I've gotten the impression," Karen said, "that they don't do that much in the way of archaeology in this area. Does Jordan work here?"

"Not all the time. Matter of fact, he's been here less and less in the past few years. When he's not on some exploration or other, he comes back to the MBL library somewhat like a homing pigeon to do the research for his next project. I haven't seen him since last December when he spent Christmas week with the rest of us at my parents' house." Susan's eyes were clouded with past visions. "God, we had fun that week. It was like the old days when Ari and Jordan were crazy eighteen-year-olds."

Karen had no idea that she was going to ask the question. "Are you in love with Jordan?"

Susan's whole body slouched with the burden of emotional pain. "As dumb as it sounds, I've been in love with that man since I was seventeen. That's why I never dated any other men seriously. They never did for me what the simplest glance from Jordan could do. I may be a jerk about it, but I'll be damned if I'll ever take second best."

Karen told herself that she was changing the subject only to help Susan up out of her gloom. Deep inside, she knew better. "Well, now I know the rest of the story about one of the three musketeers. What about Ariel? Why was your cousin raised with you like your brother?"

Susan took in a large breath and let it back out again as if to forcefully expel the bad air of frustrated love. "Ariel got the dreamy side of his nature from his father. That's also where he got those incredible eyes. I guess it was those eyes that first caught Aunt Lily's attention. According to my mother, her sister fell promptly and madly in love with Joshua Singer without a thought of what kind of life she might have with him. You see, Uncle Josh was in the merchant marine and was just as likely to spend six months on the other side of the world as here. Mom says Lily figured that after Joshua and she were married, she'd be able to convince him to leave the merchant marine. After a year of marriage, she still hadn't convinced him. So the very next time her husband was on leave, she made sure to get pregnant, thinking that a child might quell his wanderlust."

"Did it?"

Susan shook her head. "Aunt Lily's mistake was to fall in love with an image rather than a real man. If she'd loved precisely who and what Joshua was, she would have also loved what he thought and what he did, including sailing off to alien places. When Ariel was born, she allowed Uncle Josh to name him, think-

ing that he might feel even more bound to the child and
thus to her."

"I gather by the look on your face," Karen said, "that
it didn't work."

"No," Susan continued, "it didn't. Whenever Uncle
Josh came home, he'd bring fabulous gifts for his small
son and spend all his time with him. Aunt Lily had
even more heartache to contend with. Not only was her
husband away so much of the time, but when he actually did come home, he spent all of his time with Ariel
instead of with her."

Karen glanced at the half-dark sky. It had an aura of
gloom and she turned back to Susan. "Your aunt must
have been a very sad woman."

"Yes," Susan said, "but I think that, in some ways,
Joshua was a sadder man. After Aunt Lily realized that
her original plans for the reformation of Joshua Singer
were never going to pan out, she started to do a lot of
partying. I can still remember, as young as I was, the
way Aunt Lily would come sailing into our house wearing gorgeous clothes and holding Ari's hand as she
delivered him to my mother to baby-sit for the night. I
don't think my mother ever told Lily how Ariel's eyes
would fill with tears when the door closed behind his
mother. Then, one night, Lily walked out the door for
the last time. She went on a yachting party that night,
got drunk, and drowned while she was swimming."

"Oh, my dear God," Karen murmured. It was one of
the saddest things she'd ever heard. There was such a
poignancy to the story, a pathos built upon the elements of three people's love—a love that had never
reached fruition. "And so Ariel lived with you?"

"He did. That was when he was seven. But I don't
think he ever forgave his mother for dying or his father
for not coming home to stay and raise him."

"Why didn't his father do just that?" Karen asked. "Why didn't he come home to take care of his son?"

"My mother claims it was because he lived in some sort of dream world in which a son had no place," Susan paused and then went on. "But recently, I've come to another conclusion. I think Joshua Singer was too frightened of the responsibility. I also think he believed Ari would be better off living with my parents. He used to send most of his paycheck to them for Ariel and they put every cent of it away for his education. Basically, Joshua is the reason Ariel now has a doctorate in oceanography."

Karen was almost afraid to ask, since she wasn't sure she wanted to hear of any further sadness, but it was a natural question. "Is Joshua still alive?"

"He died two years ago on board a ship in the Caribbean. He had a heart attack. I can't help but think it was actually a broken heart."

Karen stood up abruptly. "Let's go back to my place and change the subject. I'm about to cry and I'd rather not."

"Me too," Susan agreed.

They paid the bill and then drove home in silence. After they had gotten Susan unpacked and settled in the guest room, the phone started to ring. Karen didn't recognize the man's voice.

"Susan," she called, "it's for you."

Karen watched Susan's face light up as she listened for a moment and then said, "Just a minute, Jordan. I'll ask her."

"Ask me what?"

Susan grinned. "Jordan says we're going fishing tomorrow afternoon and that he has a friend who'd like to go too but this friend refuses to go unless he also has a date. Jordan wants to know if you'll accept a blind date if he vouches for his friend's honorable intentions."

Karen thought briefly of what her plans for the next day were. Some laundry. Maybe a manicure. Fishing sounded much better, particularly since she'd never gone fishing in her entire life. A new experience was just what she needed, and besides, she'd like to meet the man who had captured Susan's heart.

"Sounds great." And then in a whisper, "Do you mind?"

Susan grinned and put the phone back up to her ear. "She'll go. See you tomorrow at one."

Chapter Three

"I wonder what this friend of Jordan's is like," Karen said as she stood in the doorway of the guest room while slipping a belt through the loops of her shorts.

"We'll find out in a few minutes—if they're on time," Susan said. She pulled a white sweatshirt down over the top of her skimpy bikini and then drew on a pair of cutoff jeans. "To tell you the truth, all I can think about is the fact that Jordan called and asked me out instead of asking me to come along on one of his and Ariel's escapades. It's a first, you know." She paused. "Another first is that you've gotten me calling my cousin Ariel instead of Ari. Adds dignity where there might not be any."

Karen smiled with pleasure at her friend's excitement over her first real date with Jordan. "I'm sure it won't be the last date." She looked at Susan's outfit and then down at her own. "Will this be all right for fishing?"

"Got a bathing suit underneath it just in case?"

Karen had put on a simple, one-piece suit made of slippery mauve material earlier. "Yup."

"Good," Susan said. "And the shorts and sneakers are perfect, but that T-shirt isn't enough. It gets pretty breezy out on the Sound. Take a sweater or something. And maybe a scarf for your hair."

A few minutes later, they were heading down the stairs when the doorbell rang. Saying she wanted to be the first to greet Jordan, Susan opened the door just wide enough to peek around it. "Oh, for God's sake."

Karen heard a couple of male chuckles from the other side of the door and wondered what Susan was oh-for-God's-saking about. When the door swung wide, she knew. A large, dark, mustached, and definitely handsome man stood on the threshold. Behind him stood Ariel. Karen's heart zoomed down into her stomach and then boomeranged back up into her throat as she stared openmouthed at the man she thought she'd never see again regardless of what she'd hoped.

Jordan stepped in and gave Susan a huge bear hug. "How are you, Susy-Q?"

Susan laughed as he picked her up and twirled her around. "I'm just fine . . . and I see that you still can't seem to keep away from my cousin." Jordan set her back down and she turned to Ariel. "I hope the two of you plan on behaving today. Karen isn't used to bad boys."

The smile in Ariel's eyes spread down his tanned face until he seemed to radiate joy. "Come on now, Jordan and I have outgrown that peculiar stage in our lives. We're more serious these days."

Susan pulled her mouth to the side. "That'll be the day." She turned to Karen. "Karen, this seemingly adult man is Jordan Hasan. Jordan, this is my best friend, Karen Watts. I'd call her Dr. Watts except all of us have doctor before our names and it seems both redundant and unfriendly."

Jordan came forward and shook Karen's hand. "I'd love to kiss you hello but Susan would probably swat me for bad manners and Ariel would probably jam a potato in my ear to see how long it would take for the internal pressure to blow it back out."

The remark was funny but Karen couldn't imagine why the other three laughed louder and harder than she. "Is there something more unusual about potatoes in ears than it already sounds?"

Susan brushed away tears of laughter that had skimmed down her cheeks. "Why don't we get going and you guys can tell Karen about the many uses of a spud while we're on the way?"

Not long after, they were headed toward the village of Woods Hole. Karen sat in the front with Ariel, wanting to move over next to him but pretending more interest in the story Susan was urging him to tell.

Ariel looked sideways at Karen and then back at the road. "As I remember it, spring had descended on Jordan and me rather like a green bomb during our freshman year at MIT. One Saturday, we took off for home where we found Susan looking just as twitchy as we were. Teenagers really don't know what to do with all the energy that the first real day of spring brings on. I'm not too sure whose idea it was—"

"Yours," Jordan said from the backseat, "it was definitely your idea." He laughed. "One of your better ones, too."

"I guess I'm to blame then," Ariel continued. "We decided to perform a little physics experiment concerning pressure, and for this, we required one potato, which we pilfered from the pantry. The next thing we required was a tail pipe, which my car very graciously supplied. Jordan offered the services of his diver's watch, which was capable of recording elapsed time. I jammed the potato halfway into the tail pipe, started up my car, and then the three of us sat on the front porch taking bets on how long it would be before the car shot out its potato bullet." Ariel glanced at Karen with an amazingly serious expression. "Mind you, it was all in the name of science."

Karen couldn't help but warm to the story and the man telling it. She could picture three devilish teenagers arguing and laughing over how long it would take the potato bomb to go off. "Yes, science and the alchemy of spring-adled brains."

"Right," Ariel said. "Anyway, Susan didn't know much about pressure buildup in exhaust pipes, so she bet on no more than a minute. I figured on four and Jordan decided seven was the magic number. Unfortunately, we were all wrong. After eight minutes, nothing had happened to the spud. But my uncle came out of the house to find out what the hell we were up to this time. For some reason, he didn't trust us when we were all together. When he saw us sitting there watching my car and looking too innocent, he went down the steps and out to the street, where he stood eyeing the car with, no doubt, deep suspicions. He very studiously walked around the car, inspecting it while we sat on the porch holding a collective breath. It took precisely nine and a half minutes. Too bad Uncle Pete was bending over to look beneath the rear fender."

Jordan laughed and interrupted. "I thought they only did this in cartoons, but poor Mr. Mathews actually leapt into the air when that potato came flying out of the tail pipe. Then he fell over backward and just sat there on the road looking like a disgruntled lion. When he got up and brushed the dirt from his pants with great deliberation, the three of us knew we were in deep trouble. We left in great haste and spent the rest of the day at the beach trying to figure out how to tame a lion."

By this time, Karen's eyes were spilling over with

tears of laughter. Finally collecting herself enough to speak, she looked over at Ariel, whose grin showed that he was still not above such antics. "Well, what did the lion do when you all trooped back home as you must have done?"

"Nothing."

"Impossible," Karen said.

Ariel brought the car to a stop and switched off the ignition before turning sideways in the seat to look at her. "Not really. He summoned all of us into his study before dinner and asked us what we'd done with the rest of our day. We were honest and told him we'd spent it trying to figure out how to calm down one very angry man. He said that we'd punished ourselves by worrying all day and so none of us need speak of it again. And we didn't. Besides, two weeks later Jordan had this brilliant idea that involved trout fishing."

Karen laughed. "I think I've heard that story already."

Ariel lifted his brows. "Who . . ." He swiveled to look at Susan. "You told her about the great fishing fiasco?"

"Sure did," Susan answered. "And speaking of fishing, let's do some."

When they climbed out of the car, Karen realized they were parked in front of a small marina that, a short time later, she discovered was owned by a good friend of Jordan. The man gave Jordan a set of keys and soon they were all on a small cruiser heading out into Vineyard Sound.

It was a perfect summer day to be out in a boat. The sun didn't seem quite so hot with a stiff ocean breeze blowing a fine spray of saltwater onto their skins. It had been years since Karen had been on even a small outboard motorboat, and this thirty-foot cruiser with its galley and sleeping accommodations for six seemed to her like the most luxurious yacht. She settled down in one of the deck chairs near Susan while the two men stood on the flying bridge driving the boat and arguing about where the best fishing ought to be.

Karen looked at Susan and wondered why her friend had let her face fall into troubled lines while she thought no one was watching. But the engine was too loud for Karen to be able to ask softly what was bothering Susan, and so she dismissed it. Maybe she was only squinting against the dance of sunlight on the rough water. Besides, everything seemed so perfect. Everyone was such delightful company, and in spite of her reservations about Ariel, Karen couldn't think of anyplace she'd rather be. And Susan's revelations concerning Ariel's childhood had softened Karen toward him. Whenever she looked at the full-grown, handsome man, she also saw the little boy who had cried because he'd felt abandoned.

After a while, Ariel and Jordan seemed to come to some sort of agreement over where the fish were biting and they cut the engine. Jordan dropped the anchor while Ariel came down to the deck. Karen looked up at him and was once again reminded of a slightly disheveled sea god. He stood there, his long legs covered in sun-bleached, frayed denim while his golden hair streamlined in the wind. Both her throat and stomach constricted with what she knew could easily become uncontrollable desire for this tall, rangy man. Surely, she thought, this was how Poseidon must appear; the legendary sea god couldn't be an old, gray-haired man as he was so often portrayed. No, the mythical god was certainly tall and blond, with eyes as powerful and blue as tropical waters.

When Jordan came to the rear of the boat, the two men worked with the fishing tackle while the women looked on. Susan gave an exaggerated stretch and yawn. "Ahh . . . this is the life. Two queens lolling about while their slaves do all the work."

Jordan took off his sweatshirt and tossed it to Susan. "Up off your duff, queen bee. This slave is hot, and when he's hot, he's ornery . . . and dangerous. Beer and soda's in the galley. Go fetch."

Susan stood up and made as if to step down into the galley but pivoted at the last minute and lashed out at Jordan's bare, muscular back with his sweatshirt. She was fast, but he was faster. In one swift movement, he'd grabbed the sweatshirt, pulled Susan to him, and pushed her down to the deck, where he tickled her unmercifully. "Say you're sorry, lady."

"Get off me," Susan gasped. "Pick on someone your own size!"

Jordan sat squarely on her legs. "Apologize for maltreatment of the slave." He reached once again for Susan's ribs.

Karen glanced over at Ariel and found that he wasn't even watching the deck show. He was calmly setting two trolling rods in holders on either side of the back of the boat as if he didn't hear the screeching laughter going on behind him. When she looked back at Jordan and Susan, Karen felt her color deepen and she quickly looked away again. Jordan was still astride Susan, but he was no longer tickling her, nor was she laughing. They were just staring at each other with every line of their faces radiating a raw desire.

Karen stood up and walked over to Ariel. "Can I do anything to help?"

He secured the second rod and then turned to her. "Yes. You can tell me that you're not mad at me anymore."

She knew what he was referring to, but she pretended innocence. "Why should I be mad at you?"

"Because I tried to rush you into something that you either didn't want or weren't ready for. I told you I was sorry almost a week ago and I'd like to say it again. I'm sorry."

He was too beautiful and somehow too vulnerable not to like, not to desire. And his eyes were too probing to lie to. "I'm sorry about it too, Ariel. The things I said to you weren't really directed at you."

"Then who were they meant for?"

"I'm not sure," Karen said quietly. "Maybe me. Maybe I've just spent too much time being an achiever and competing with men in what is still a man's profession to be able to submit myself to the male opponent."

Ariel slipped his arm around her shoulders and drew her close to him. "It's not really a matter of submitting to a man, you know. By the sound of it, I'd say it's more a matter of submitting to yourself."

Karen looked away. She felt suddenly shy from such a concise and revealing conversation, but when her eyes came to rest on Jordan and Susan, she looked swiftly back to Ariel to find that he was staring with interest at his friend and his cousin. They were no longer just gazing raptly into each other's eyes; they were locked in each other's arms, engrossed in a passionate kiss.

Ariel dropped his arm away from Karen, walked over to the prone couple, and gave Jordan a sturdy kick in the rear. "Cut it out, you villainous Arab. You're on the verge of being obscene."

Jordan lifted his head away from Susan, and Karen could see the drugged look on his face. "Huh? Oh, hell!" He grinned. "Can't you mind your own business?"

"Usually," Ariel flung down at his friend, "but if you

two keep this up, you'll be doing what two people aren't supposed to do in public. Besides, I can't watch the lines and drive the boat at the same time."

Jordan took a deep breath, got off Susan, and helped her to her feet. "Heck . . . I thought I'd just caught myself a prize fish right here on deck."

"Later, old buddy, later." Ariel gave Susan a narrow-eyed look. "Stay away from the Arab until we've caught our dinner."

Susan saluted him. "Aye, aye, cap'n."

Fifteen minutes later, Jordan was up on the bridge driving the boat at low speed while Ariel and Susan took turns watching the lines trailing behind. Karen wasn't asked to watch, since she'd never gone fishing before and wasn't really sure she could tell when there was a strike. It didn't take long before a striped bass was reeled in, and it also didn't take long for Karen to realize that she couldn't stand seeing a fish with a hook in its mouth. She got up from the chair and climbed up to the bridge to join Jordan where she wouldn't have to look at jaws that gaped and bled.

"I hope Susan and I didn't embarrass you," Jordan said as she joined him.

"Not really," Karen lied, "though I must admit I was afraid you were about to."

Jordan laughed. "I almost embarrassed myself. It never dawned on me before just how nice it might be to sit on Susan."

Karen grinned at him. She could see what it was that attracted Susan to this man. There was something so free-spirited in him. "You really are somewhat of a lecher, aren't you?"

Jordan shook his head. "Not where Susan is concerned. She's been a buddy of mine for too long." He paused and looked out across the great expanse of water. "Much too long. It's time to stop being just buddies."

Great! Karen shouted to herself. Aloud, she said, "You've had a lot of good times with Susan and Ariel, haven't you?"

Jordan turned and looked at her and then on past her and down to the deck where Susan was tossing the fish into the bait well. "More than just good times. Ariel and Susan have been my home away from home. I've always thought of them as my brother and sister . . . until just a little while ago. I don't think I can have Susan as a sister anymore." He scratched his head. "Only thing is, I'm gone too much of the time to have her as anything else. She can't just be another woman in another port." He slammed his hand down on the steering wheel. "Damn!"

His dilemma was obvious to Karen, but she really didn't know what to say to him. The whole thing reminded her of the story Susan had told her the night before about Ariel's merchant-marine father and his frustrated mother. She didn't want to see that happen to Susan.

An hour later there were five fish in the bait well, enough for dinner. By then, Ariel had replaced Jordan on the bridge, and when he saw the last fish pulled in, he cut the engines and climbed down to drop anchor. Coming to the back of the boat, he announced, "No sense in killing what we can't eat. Why don't we pack up the gear and sit around until our skin burns off?"

"Sounds good to me," Jordan said. "One small reminder, however, before we get too lazy to think about it." He turned to Karen. "Both Susan and Ariel know about this, though I'm sure it doesn't hurt to remind them." He pointed to a small red button just beneath the lid of the bait well. "If you sit on top of the well, make sure you don't hit this button. It releases the trap door and those five little fishies we caught will go back from whence they came."

"I think," Karen said, "that I'll simply refrain from sitting on the bait well."

"Good," Jordan replied, "since it happens to be my favorite place to sit." He eased himself down onto the cushions and turned sideways to look behind him where the shore was a thin line on the horizon.

Karen was still staring at the button, thinking that it was a lousy place for such an important thing, when she saw Jordan cross one leg over the other. His foot was awfully close to the little red button. She was about to mention it to him, but she never got the chance. He wiggled his foot and his heel made hard contact with the button.

No one said anything. They all stared at Jordan, whose face showed nothing other than complete disbelief at what he'd just done. Then Ariel rose slowly from his chair and took the two necessary steps to reach Jordan, who was himself on the rise. Karen tried to read Ariel's face, but she could see no emotion there. He lifted his arms, planted them flat on Jordan's chest, and shoved. Only he shoved a little too hard and lost his balance. Suddenly, Ariel and Jordan were sailing over the side of the boat.

Susan didn't laugh as the ocean spouted up around the men—she howled and then stopped just long enough to yell, "Men overboard!" before hooting and howling again.

Karen didn't know whether to laugh or be scared. "Susan, they need help!"

Susan stood up, still spilling out her mirth. "They sure as hell do!"

Karen stepped with Susan to the back of the boat and

looked down. Both Ariel and Jordan were swimming
back up to the side with grins that took up most of the
space on their handsome faces. "Don't just stand there,
ladies," Jordan called. "Help this moron and his venge-
ful friend back on board."

"Can you swim?" Ariel said, looking up at Karen.

"Not well enough for these waters."

"Too bad." He took her offered hand as he planted a
foot on the side of the boat, using his leg as a fulcrum to
swing up and over the rail.

"Why's it too bad?" she asked, trying desperately not
to glance down where she knew his wet jeans clutched
at his body—everywhere.

He bent down to her, his lips a tantalizing whisper
away. "Because I know this great game called revel-in-
the-deep."

His suggestive comment sent her back a step and she
watched with feigned interest as Susan helped Jordan
back into the boat. He stood there, his mustache comic-
ally drooping. "I guess we'll either have to start all over
again or I'm elected to buy us all dinner."

"You win the election," Ariel said. "I don't feel like
fishing anymore."

Jordan scanned Ariel's face. "You're not going to
turn grouchy on us, are you?"

"Not in the least. I have better things to do." Ariel
lunged at Karen and wrapped her in a cold, drenching
hug.

"Cut it out," Karen yelled at him. "I feel like I'm tangled up in a glob of seaweed." It was far from the truth,
but she could hardly admit, even to herself, that a wet
T-shirt on a woman couldn't hold a candle to Ariel's wet
clothes clinging to the long, hard contours of his body.

Ariel released her and looked down her damp length.
"Excellent. You're a mess. The only one who isn't a

wreck now is my sister-cousin." He turned to Jordan. "Remedy the situation, you scroungy old sea dog."

"With pleasure," was Jordan's answer as he pulled a willing Susan against his chest.

Karen was immediately struck by the sight of Susan disappearing in the big man's arms. She was also struck once again by their passion being held in check by only the thinnest of threads. She slid her eyes sideways and up. Ariel was not smiling as she had believed he would be; he was serious, thoughtful.

"You two are a disgrace," Ariel announced as he stepped up to the couple and forcefully separated them. He grinned at Jordan. "Passion in public rarely pans out in private."

Jordan drove his thick dark brows together and scowled at his blond friend. Then his brows relaxed again as he began chuckling. "You should know."

"Care for another swim?" Ariel asked.

Jordan held up his palm. "Whoa, boy. I didn't say anything."

"I didn't think so either." Ariel walked away toward the front of the cruiser. "I'll get the anchor and drive us back to the marina since you'll be buying dinner—a good, expensive dinner."

Karen thought briefly about this exchange between the two men, wondering if Ariel had once made a public display of passion. After a tiny and annoying burst of jealousy, she dismissed it with the sudden understanding that these men spent half their time together happily teasing each other. This teasing was the only method they had of saying, "I love you."

The sun was low in the sky by the time, wet and faintly fishy, they piled into Ariel's car, where they all sat for a moment working out the logistics of the coming evening. It was decided that Ariel would drop Jordan off at the efficiency apartment he kept in Woods Hole, take the women back to Karen's house, and then drive out to his cottage. He'd be back to pick up everyone at eight.

"I'd say," Susan stated as they closed the door behind them in Karen's house, "that you and Ariel had more than just professional contact that day you examined his eyes."

"What makes you think that?" Karen knew she was hedging, but she couldn't bring herself to discuss Ariel with Susan.

"I think it was the way you looked at each other." Susan started up the stairs, then stopped. "Karen, as much as I love my cousin, I love you too. Be careful with him." She turned and sat down on the first step. "It's hard to explain. Ariel's not what they call a womanizer, but well, some of the things he does could make him seem that way. I don't think I've ever seen him date a woman for more than a few weeks . . . except for one." She shook her head. "But that doesn't count."

"What doesn't count?" Karen asked.

Susan looked at her for so long that Karen thought her friend had lost the conversational track. "What doesn't count, Susan?"

"It's just going to make Ariel seem absolutely awful in your eyes and that's something I don't want to do. Besides, I never really knew what went on between him and Nicole."

"This is ridiculous," Karen grumbled. "Either you tell me everything or you say nothing whatsoever. Don't throw out teasers."

Susan slapped her thighs decisively. "Okay, but let's head upstairs and start getting ready. We can talk while we change."

Susan followed her into her bedroom, where Karen

stood in front of her open closet trying to choose an appropriate outfit for the restaurant in Woods Hole that had been chosen. Casual but not grubby was Ariel's pronouncement on how they should all dress. "I can listen while I pick out my clothes," she said.

"Right." Susan's single word was filled with unhappy resignation. "When I think back on it, I'm not sure whether or not to classify it as one of Ari's interminable pranks, since it was Jordan who introduced him to Nicole. Where Jordan met her, I can't imagine, nor do I want to. You see, Nicole was a French lady of the night."

The dress Karen had pulled from the closet for inspection slipped through her fingers and fell to her feet unnoticed. "A what?"

"You know. The oldest profession in the world?" Susan took in Karen's colorless face and rushed on. "I don't even know if he paid her or if they were lovers or friends or what the hell they were to each other. All I know is that Ari spent a lot of time with her, according to a mutual friend living in the same apartment building as Nicole. Somehow, Dad got whiff of it and then made the huge mistake of telling Mom. She hit the roof, and luckily or unluckily, Ariel's father was in port and she went to him with the story. From what I can glean, Uncle Josh had a talk with his son but no one knows what was said. All we know is that Ariel stopped seeing Nicole."

In her mind, Karen could see a smooth stone heart resting in her palm. "How old was Ariel at the time?"

Susan gazed out the window in silent calculation. "It was in the fall . . . yes, the fall when Ariel had just entered MIT. He was still eighteen."

A very special lady, he'd told her, had given him the stone heart when he was eighteen. Karen wondered if that special lady had been named Nicole. So what? she asked herself. So what if he'd been involved with such a woman? It had happened over thirteen years ago. That was a long time. Then she remembered what Susan had said about Jordan's part in it. "Does it bother you that Jordan was involved with this woman also?"

"Not really. It was years ago. Besides, if that sort of thing bothered me, what do you suppose it would do to me if I dwelt too much on the fact that he probably has, as they say, a woman in every port right now?"

"I guess you're right." But maybe there was something that Susan ought to think about. "While you and Ariel were fishing, I kept company with Jordan for a short time up on the bridge and we had a brief conversation concerning the two of you. I think you should hear it."

Susan's eyes narrowed. "What did he say?"

Karen repeated as much of the conversation with Jordan as she could remember and then added, "He's upset, Susan. I don't think he knows quite what to do about you."

Susan laughed happily. "I've already got it all figured out. I've been working on it for a long time." She looked mischievously at Karen. "But I'm not going to tell you. Wouldn't do to count all those marvelous chickens before they're hatched."

Karen looked at her friend's happy face, and her mind superimposed the troubled expression she'd glimpsed on Susan at the beginning of their fishing trip. She mentioned it and Susan smiled sheepishly.

"Oh, it was just a short episode of doubt concerning Jordan's motives. For a little while, I had the feeling that Ariel had put him up to asking me out just so my cousin could be with you."

The next hour was spent in showering and dressing, with little time left for talking. But Karen found that getting ready for dinner took very little mental strain, and so her mind remained occupied with thoughts of Ariel: Ariel as a small child with virtually no parents; Ariel as an older child talking with a gray-haired marine biologist on a Boston beach; Ariel at eighteen with a French "lady"; Ariel and Jordan launching themselves from one devilish episode into another; Ariel standing in her office doorway like a sea god; Ariel kissing her on the beach making her feel that the lightning of the sky came from the electricity being switched on within her; and Ariel standing on the deck of the cruiser apologizing for having tried to rush her into physical love.

She weighed each and every piece of knowledge on an emotional scale, and no matter how logical she tried to be about it, the scale seesawed first one way and then the other. The only thing she was sure about was that she couldn't wait to see him again.

"And that probably makes you a damned fool," she whispered to herself in the mirror. "For a brainy woman, you're feeling awfully silly about a man."

She looked at the image she'd created and her reflection showed her inner confusion. Without realizing what she was doing, she'd chosen extremely tailored white slacks, plain flat sandals, and her usual upswept hairstyle of a sophisticated swirl. But the blouse she wore was not plain, or severe, nor was it sophisticated; it was a luscious drape of royal-blue silk with the triangular opening slicing down to a point barely above her cleavage. The thoroughly feminine aura of the blouse was in sharp contrast to the masculine lines of everything else. It was striking, but then, so was the subtle battle that had persisted within her for years, the war between her driving intelligence and her soft, feminine yearnings. If only she had been a little bit more like her sister, and if only Liza had drawn off a few of Karen's more levelheaded qualities, then a perfect balance might have been achieved, she thought wistfully.

Her musings were cut off by the ring of the doorbell, and a short time later, Karen felt the warmth of Ariel's long leg pressed casually against her own as she sat next to him in the restaurant's plush booth. She wondered if he knew that he was doing it, and then she wondered if he knew what he was capable of doing to her just by touching her with his eyes.

The nautical atmosphere of the restaurant was augmented by the crowds of people filled with vacationtime spirit, and this spirit was combined with the buoyant mood of her three companions, putting Karen at ease. She sat back quietly after they had eaten to ponder the three people she was with. All owners of the highest educational degree in their fields, just as she was, they were nevertheless different from her. They didn't seem to concern themselves with how they sounded or looked. They didn't seem to care whether or not they came across as smart people. But how do you turn off your intelligence? she asked herself.

The conversation swung about wildly, traveling from tales of deep-sea treasures recounted by Jordan, to Susan's seriously told story of extracting a huge emerald from the nose of an elegant lady who swore her to secrecy without ever revealing the cause of such a predicament. Then Ariel spun out some of the many yarns concerning *Alvin,* the small submersible operated by the nearby oceanographic institution. Karen laughed with abandon over Ariel's story about the time an audacious swordfish had boldly attacked Alvin only to get his "sword" stuck in one of the little submarine's seams. On that night, the scientists and crew members enjoyed swordfish steaks for dinner.

By the time they'd finished their coffee, a band had begun playing, drawing Jordan and Susan out onto the dance floor. Ariel turned his attention away from Jordan, who was holding Susan as close as he could while barely moving to the music. "I'd ask you to dance, only I don't think you'd enjoy it. I think my legs are too long or something. Anyway, it's not among my accomplishments."

"That's okay. It's not among mine either." She glanced at Jordan and Susan and noticed that Jordan's hand had slid down her back almost to a place where his hand shouldn't be while the two were in a public place. "I understand that this is Susan's first real date with Jordan."

Ariel looked at the couple and smirked. "I feel like a chubby little boy wearing nothing but wings who shoots arrows into people when they least expect it."

"What do you mean?"

Ariel looked back at Karen with only the smile in his eyes showing. "Remember Monday night when I told you that I'm as relentless as a molecule of ocean water?"

Karen colored slightly at the memory of why he'd talked about water molecules traveling around the world. "I remember."

"Well, I set this whole thing up. Jordan was waiting at my place when I got home that night, and after we'd gone through the usual formalities of telling each other what we've been up to for the past few months, he asked me where I'd been for the last half-hour. I told him I'd been with a beautiful lady who'd rejected me."

"Ariel, I didn't—"

"Yes you did. But that's not important anyway. Then he asked me if I was going to do anything about it and it was then that the scheme came to me— well, it was more like a mystical vision. I had him call Susan and ask her down for Saturday, figuring she'd call on you for a place to stay. I guess you can see the way I had it all planned. Worked out perfectly, too."

Karen felt a tiny knot of anger form in her chest. Susan's suspicions had been well-founded. "You mean you used your best friend and your cousin for your own purposes?"

Ariel glanced at the dance floor and then back at Karen. "Yes, but Jordan was fully aware of what I was doing, and at this point, I think Susan would rather thank me than clobber me. She's been in love with him for years."

"What makes you think so?"

Ariel shook his head. "See the look on her face right now? She's had that look since the first day I brought him home with me." He slipped his arm around Karen's shoulders and brushed her hair with his lips. "Now, if I could only get you to look at me like that."

Karen could feel the immediate response his whispered touch created, but she was afraid to let it expand within her, and more than that, she was afraid to respond to this man in particular. Susan had warned her that Ariel was not the serious sort with women. Karen used the only weapon against emotion that she'd ever had: words.

"I won't let you play with me like you've played with Susan and Jordan."

Ariel's lips curved in a gentle smile before he leaned close and said in a hushed voice, "I don't always play. Sometimes I work hard and sometimes I want to make love to a woman . . . like right now."

Karen pulled away from him, and her instinct for emotional survival spurred her on. "Why can't we just have an intelligent relationship?"

The smile in Ariel's eyes was gone. "Because intelligence, with its cold analysis and synthesis, is not all there is to life. And it's certainly not the only thing that makes for a healthy male-female relationship."

Karen took his words as a personal attack. "Well, you can't expect me to just shuck off all my intellect and learning and act like an idiot as you, Jordan, and Susan obviously enjoy doing!" She was the idiot. While she was cutting him with words, her body was revealing the truth. She couldn't control the press of her leg against his, couldn't control the ache that the warmth of his body created in her mind and loins.

Ariel responded in a barely controlled voice. "If idiotic is your way of describing hard play, then, yes, that's what we like doing." Karen opened her mouth to speak, but he continued. "None of us is stupid, Karen. Susan didn't get to be an otolaryngologist with any less ease than you got your degree. And Jordan's abilities have put him in demand all over the world. I also very humbly submit that I've had a few exceptional job offers because of my own particular expertise."

For the first time in her life, Karen felt stupid, truly lacking. Seasoning this, and perhaps more lethal, was a feminine ego that had been in a sad state as far back as she could recall, and that damaged ego had just received another kick. Ariel had made it clear that three highly intelligent people could still lead complete lives. They could successfully juggle the mental strain of their careers with playful abandonment and—she looked at Susan and Jordan kissing on the dance floor—hard loving.

Then Greg crossed her mind. "Look, having been married once, I learned something that I'll never forget: love and play just aren't all they're cracked up to be."

Ariel was too quick. He'd seen her glance at Jordan and Susan and he'd seen the pain scatter like shards of glass in her eyes.

"Just because you married a man who probably didn't know any more about women than that they're somehow different from men doesn't mean it's time to turn sour on the greatest part of life. And it sure as hell shouldn't be enough to make you run off with your tail between your legs every time someone suggests playing with you."

"Playing?" Karen felt her control sliding into oblivion. "Just playing? Is that your idea of what making love is all about?" He made as if to speak, but she wouldn't let him. "Don't deny it. That's really what this is all about. You tried to get me into your bed last Monday, and then, when it didn't pan out, you worked up a scheme to try again. Now that I see what's going on and fully understand your shallow attitude toward sex, I wouldn't even put it past you to have plotted with Jordan to keep Susan busy with him while you tried to work your admittedly considerable charms on me. But it's not enough, Ariel. At this point, you'd have to use a . . . a crowbar to get between my legs!"

She'd never before used a phrase quite so vulgar, and Karen turned her face away from Ariel to hide the flush of shame. Feeling him shift away from her, she looked back to see him swinging his legs out of the booth. He stood up, walked onto the dance floor, and spoke briefly with Susan and Jordan before returning to the table.

Even though she was blinded by her own angry confusion, Karen was still aware of the graceful way his body moved. He wore a soft, maroon jersey shirt that was unbuttoned halfway down his chest to ward off the midsummer heat, and the fabric of his light-gray slacks clung to his long, strong thighs and seemed to almost kiss the extended back of his calves as he walked toward her. Incongruously, she wondered where he bought his clothes, where he managed to find a store that sold pants for a man with such long legs. The only thing she was not aware of was how her body showed every nuance of her thoughts. Her pupils were dilated, she was running her tongue along her slightly parted lips, and her entire torso inched at an ever-increasing angle across the table toward Ariel.

Ariel remained standing beside the table, coldly observing her for a moment before he said, "I'm going to take you home."

The car skidded on a patch of windblown sand. Ariel took his foot off the accelerator, regained control, then drove the last mile safely home by reminding himself of what an eighty-mile-an-hour accident could do to a man's face.

He was still thinking about faces when he climbed out of the car. So many meanings in a face. Karen's face, Karen's beautiful face so filled with fear and lust at the same time. Why? Well, he'd be damned if he was going to question the lust.

He turned toward the ocean, not able to see it in the blackness, but able to hear it. The waves sounded powerful tonight, thrusting against the beach, mating with the shore. . . .

Ariel laughed out loud. If he didn't have a woman soon, he was going to do something he'd regret—like trying to ravish a sand dune. He laughed again, a mirthless sound. It wasn't just any woman he wanted, it was Karen. What the hell was the matter with her? Or him, for that matter? Every other woman he'd ever wanted had practically thrown herself at his feet.

He sat down, then lay back right where he was, mindless of the sand creeping beneath the waistband of his slacks. For a long time, he lay motionless, remembering what Karen had said about competing in a man's world and about submitting to a man. Was that what scared her? Submitting?

Ariel let out a string of curses, felt better, then grinned. He'd said some of those same words the first time he'd met Nicole and she'd said that even if she *had* been considering him as a bed partner—which she wasn't—his language would have wiped the thought right out of her mind. He'd reddened right down to his eighteen-year-old toes. He'd used obscene language because he'd thought that was what you were *supposed* to do with a . . . Even in his private thoughts, Ariel couldn't bring himself to use the word so many others had applied to Nicole. Those people had been wrong. Nicole was a teacher, a very special kind of teacher. She had her own peculiar brand of morals. If a man was hardly more than a kid, she wouldn't take his money. She wouldn't go to bed with him either. She said that if she could only teach every young man how to love a woman and how to *make* love to a woman, then her profession would go bankrupt.

Ariel scratched absently at his waist. Had he forgotten the things Nicole had taught him? How could he? She'd often said he was the best student she'd ever had. He had a natural talent for picking up the smallest nuances in a person's expression. And he was practically a genius at playing roles, Nicole's method of gaining access to another person's mind by pretending to *be* that person.

Ariel sat up. That was it! If he could just get Karen to step outside of herself, to imagine herself as someone else, maybe she'd lose that fear.

Submission. What kind of person would either freely submit or be forced to do so? A prisoner.

Ariel stood up quickly, then groaned. Nicole had also told him that many woman hated the look of white Jockey shorts, and he'd worn none since, white or otherwise. Now he stood with at least a zillion grains of sand in his pants. He unzipped his slacks, let them drop down around his ankles, brushed at himself, then groaned again. He was fully aroused.

Must have been the idea of Karen as my prisoner, he thought. Me and my great big ideas. When he realized he was grinning stupidly into the dark night, he stepped out of his pants, picked them up, and walked into his cottage.

I'll take a shower. A very cold shower. Perfectly lousy idea, Ariel. Lukewarm will do just fine. No sense in being a damned masochist about it.

Chapter Four

❧

Karen stifled a yawn as she led the young man back into the examining room. Sunday night had contained no more sleep than Saturday night had. Ariel had left her abruptly at the door and she'd gone directly to bed. Susan had not shown up at all during the night, nor had she returned until midafternoon on Sunday. Karen had refused to tell Susan about the argument with Ariel, and Susan had left for Boston too happy about Jordan to notice Karen's silence.

Putting herself on automatic, she indicated to the very young Mr. Rivera that he should sit in the examining chair. He was another referral of Dr. Singer's. Ariel. Because of him, she'd spent all of Sunday cleaning her house from top to bottom in an attempt to work off what she assured herself was anger. But after Susan had left and after there just wasn't anything left to clean, Karen had walked into the examining room in which she presently stood. She'd looked around at the cold, sterile instruments, and she'd let the tears of regret and yearning fall unchecked.

Karen looked at Manuel Rivera as he sat fidgeting in the chair. While she was noting his black eye, which was obviously several days old, and while she was wondering how he'd gotten it, she was also remembering the various things Susan had told her about Ariel.

Though her friend had mentioned characteristics that should indicate to Karen that his viewpoint of women was, at best, a light one, it was not this aspect of the man on which she now found herself dwelling. She knew without a doubt that she'd hurt him. She'd rejected not only his sexual overtures but also his philosophy and the very essence of the friendships he had with his cousin and Jordan.

Karen sat down on the high stool she'd drawn up close to the examining chair, and as she heard herself asking the slight-bodied patient about his eye, she also heard another question, the one she'd asked Susan about how Ariel had come to be raised as her brother. It was the answer to that question that continued to haunt her; it was the vision of a small boy with tears in his eyes as he watched his mother abandon him yet another time so that she could go to a party. He was a man now, but she knew with some sixth sense that the little boy still lived somewhere within Ariel. She also knew that she'd as good as slapped the face of that sad child.

Karen had to tug herself back up from her painful thoughts in order to hear what Manuel Rivera was saying. One part of her wanted to revel in the guilt; another part wanted to get away from it, to think of anything but the callous words she'd flung at Ariel while they'd sat in the restaurant.

"Most dockworkers are okay," he was saying, "but this one guy has been on my case for weeks. After *Alvin*'s catamaran, *Lulu,* was in and tied up for the night and almost everyone was gone, I went down to the dock just to look at the ship." In spite of his black eye, Manuel gave a wistful look. "Someday, I'll go out on *Lulu* and maybe even down in *Alvin.*"

"Anyway, to make a long story short, this one guy

called me a spick and I took a swing at him. Stupid. Dockworkers are strong." He indicated his eye. "This was the result."

Karen turned down the lights and flicked on her small flashlight. Only to calm the twenty-three-year-old whose hands obviously shook, she asked, "What do your friends call you, Mr. Rivera?"

"Manny."

"Well, then, Manny, tell me a little about yourself. You have an accent—you're not originally from the States, are you?" She beamed the light first into his uninjured right eye.

"I'm from Puerto Rico. A lot of hard work and scholarships have gotten me all the way to the institution for graduate studies . . . and a black eye."

"It mustn't have been easy." Karen leaned back on her stool. "I assume you occasionally use microscopes, right?" He nodded. "And you never use your right eye?"

Both of Manny's eyes seemed black in the twilight darkness of the room. "Yeah. When I was a little kid, I thought no one saw more than blurry shapes with their right eye. It wasn't until I was eight that they discovered that stupid optic nerve."

Karen was now nervous herself. The optic nerve in his right eye, the one that hadn't been blackened, was misshapen for whatever reasons. Perhaps it had happened before birth or maybe during. It made no difference. The damage was irreparable and he'd always be partially blind in one eye. It wasn't that specific problem which now worried her. Rather, it was the realization that the good sight in his left eye was imperative. She remembered how he'd bumped into the chair before sitting down.

"Before I take a look at your left eye, Manny, tell me about it."

Manny explained how, when the swelling had gone down, he'd discovered what seemed like a cloud obscuring part of his visual field.

Karen began her examination of the injured eye and was silent while she worked, except for an explanation of the drops of tropicamide she'd placed in his eyes to dilate the pupils.

The examination was done. That had been the easy part. Now she had to tell Manny what she'd found. She turned up the lights, thankful that she'd had a dimmer switch installed. There was pain enough ahead for this sweet young man without submitting him to the harsh glare of lights with his presently dilated pupils.

How did she tell someone who had only one good eye that that eye would also be lost without immediate surgery? She decided to lead up to it by using her plastic model of the eye to explain the position, composition, and vital function of the retina—and what happened when there was a small break in the upper half: detachment of the retina would progress quickly, until he was blind.

Later, Karen sat at her kitchen table staring at a rapidly cooling plate of hash and eggs. She noted how the butter was congealing into translucent yellow blobs and she shoved the dish away in disgust. The tight ball of fear in her stomach had erased any desire to eat. Over and over again, she heard herself telling Manny that he had a detached retina, that surgery was imperative, and that if it wasn't done immediately, he'd be blind for life.

She had used strong, clear words in an attempt to make Manny understand his serious condition, but she hadn't meant to scare the wits out of him. Why hadn't she been gentler, more quietly persuasive? Like a broken video disk, Manny's reaction replayed itself, going from the beginning right through to the end and then back to the beginning again. As she sat there, Karen saw the terror spreading across Manny Rivera's smooth, dark features. She saw his hands turn white as he gripped the arms of the examining chair. She heard him shout "No!" and saw him bolt out of the chair toward the door. And she felt herself reaching out to grab his arm, her fingers closing on empty air because, within seconds, he'd managed to escape the examining room, race through the waiting room, and fly out into the street. By the time Karen had gotten to the door leading outside, Manny was nowhere in sight.

Karen got up from the kitchen chair, picked up her full dish of food, and scraped every last crumb down into the garbage-disposal unit. She'd have to find Manny. She knew from his medical record that he lived in Woods Hole. If he wasn't listed in the phone book, then she'd just have to drive to his place. She was about to go to the directory when the doorbell rang.

Filled with thoughts of finding Manny, she opened the front door and was shocked to see him standing there, but even more shocked when she noticed the man standing behind him.

"I know it's after office hours," Ariel said quietly as he put a protective arm around Manny's slender shoulders, "but I figured that, under the circumstances, you wouldn't mind. May we come in, Dr. Watts?"

On the periphery of her mind, Karen noticed Ariel's use of the formal "Dr. Watts" and wondered briefly if he'd relegated her back into that position after their date on Saturday. She looked at Manny. "I'm glad you changed your mind, I was just about to try to find you."

Ariel gently shoved Manny through the door. "Manny's still a little reluctant, but maybe, between you and me, we can convince him."

Karen quickly slipped into her professional envelope. "Let's go into the office."

She led the two men into her examining room, where she indicated the chair in front of her desk to Manny while she sat down in one on the other side. Ariel pulled up the tall stool she used during exams. She glanced quickly at his long legs and then away. His feet reached the floor, something hers could not do.

Ariel, sitting higher as he was, seemed to be presiding over the small drama. "Manny, why don't you tell Dr. Watts the things that are bothering you?" He shifted his gaze to Karen and his eyes seemed to be prying into her mind when he added, "As a doctor, she's open to you both physically and mentally."

Manny shifted in the chair and hung his dark head so that all Karen could see were shiny black waves.

"Manny," she said softly, "Dr. Singer is right. I've been thinking and worrying about you ever since this afternoon. Please talk to me."

Without looking up, Manny said, "I don't know what to talk about."

"Yes you do," Ariel cut in. "Just tell the doctor what you told me."

Manny looked up at Ariel, and Karen could see the pleading in his dark eyes. Ariel stared back with a surprising mixture of intensity, humor, and gentleness. But it was to Karen that he spoke. "I found Manny on my doorstep this evening. He apparently walked the whole way after he left here." Still staring into Manny's eyes, he added, "Though, for a ride in my sports car, I'd think it would have been easier just to call me on the telephone."

Manny grinned and Karen let out a breath she hadn't known she'd been holding. Ariel had broken some of the tension.

"I'm sorry I ran out on you, Dr. Watts." Manny was now looking directly at her. "You have no idea how scared I was."

"I think I do, Manny." Did she? How would she know what it was like to be told you're bordering on blindness?

Manny glanced at Ariel and then back at Karen. "I told Dr. Singer about what you'd found in my eye and he said you could fix it . . . you didn't tell me that."

"You never gave me a chance."

"Even if I had, I probably would have run anyway."

"Why?"

"It's just scary. Only one good eye and that one failing rapidly. I have no money to pay you and what family I've got is way the hell down in Puerto Rico. It's pretty upsetting to be going blind all alone."

Karen spoke past a lump in her throat. "You're not going blind. And you're not alone, since you've obviously got Dr. Singer in your camp—and you've got me too."

For the next hour they talked until Manny believed that all his problems, present and future, had been solved. When the question arose of how the hospital bill would be paid, since Manny had no medical insurance, Karen and Ariel looked quickly at each other and a message skimmed between them. Together, they assured Manny that there was no problem there either. He was still too distraught to realize that money *was* a problem.

Ariel followed Manny out the waiting room door, but turned back for a moment. Karen was instantly reminded of the first time she'd seen him standing in that very doorway. He looked little different from the way he had then, only this time he wore ragged cutoffs and Indian sandals that exposed the length of his legs.

Karen pulled her eyes up from his strong, tanned thighs as he said softly, "You're quite a woman, Karen. What's hidden that fact from you?" Then the door was closing and he was gone.

Karen. Out of Manny's earshot, he'd used her first name. And come to think of it, she'd called him Dr. Singer in the office. With this thought, she realized that Ariel had been emphasizing the fact that she was a doctor before being a woman so that Manny might gain some badly needed confidence in her abilities. Suddenly, she wondered where she was going to scrape up her own confidence. She'd repaired torn retinas before, but never on a person who had only one good eye to begin with. There was no room for error here. One slip with the laser she'd be using on his eye—a sneeze, a jerk of her hand—and Manny would be virtually blind for life.

Karen sat for a long time in one of the office chairs pondering her own abilities. She was a general ophthalmologist, not specially trained for eye surgery as Greg had been.

Karen walked into the small office usually occupied by Fran, lifted the phone from its cradle, and dialed a number she knew by heart. It rang just once before she hung up. Why was she trying to call Greg? Because she was scared, she realized, scared of operating on Manny, scared of the loneliness she was feeling. But it wasn't Greg she needed, it was Ariel.

Karen stood up and walked resolutely from the office, telling herself it was absurd to believe she needed a man whom she'd known for only a week. So she went to her kitchen phone and dialed Susan. Susan wasn't home. Sighing in exasperation, she redialed Greg's number. But he wasn't home either.

She had no one to talk with. Well, so what? She'd

never had anyone to talk with, she told herself firmly. Her radiologist father had always been as negative as the X rays he stared at all day. And her gynecologist mother knew everything about feminine anatomy but very little about her own two daughters.

A mental image of Ariel taunted her mind and Karen leaned against the wall, looking at her hospital-clean kitchen. It was a perfect kitchen created by a woman driven toward perfection. Yet she felt far from perfect.

Ariel looked at the clock on the wall of the Marine Biological Laboratory's library. Midnight. What the hell was he doing at the MBL when he could be home in bed where he belonged? Why was he reading this journal article on a subject in which he was already well-versed? Metamorphosis, he thought. Some of those tropical fish really had it all figured out.

Ariel leaned his elbow on the desk and cupped his chin in his hand as he stared once again at the picture of an indigo hamlet, perhaps the happiest fish in the world. He smiled as he thought of this particular creature's exotic sex life. It was a hermaphrodite of the highest order. Late in the afternoon, a pair of hamlets would court each other to determine which would be the egg-releasing female. The dominant one would win this role. When all was decided, they'd spawn. Then, as weird as it sounded, they'd spawn again, only this time, they'd switch roles, the female turning into the male and vice versa. They could alternate in this way as many as five times in a single mating.

The picture faded as a vision of Karen floated into his mind. Ariel suddenly found himself wondering if Karen had ever actually experienced the female role. Though she was both beautiful and feminine, she seemed unaware of herself as a woman, almost as if she'd refused to acknowledge that side of herself. Maybe, just maybe, he could help her to realize her own femininity.

Karen walked into the operating room two days later at eleven in the morning. She was scrubbed, masked, and gowned. Physically ready. But psychologically she didn't feel ready at all. Not that she hadn't tried. She'd spent all her free time in the last two days reviewing all her old textbooks.

Somehow, she'd worked the miracle of reserving an operating room, even though the summer months had brought a burgeoning population not only to the Cape, but also to its hospitals.

She'd called Ariel with the hospital-admittance time and information because Manny was staying with him. Ariel was not going to give the frightened young man another chance to run. He was even going to bring Manny to the hospital Wednesday morning.

Now, as Karen walked over to Manny, who lay stretched out on the operating table, she had an incongruous thought, one that was at first repugnant to her and then frightening: if she made a mistake, would Manny still be expected to pay the hospital?

She looked down at the calmly drugged face of Manuel Rivera, smiled, and said, "Hi."

Karen had no idea of the time, nor did she care. She walked back out of the operating room, peeling off and discarding her gloves as she went. She stood for a moment in the light-green corridor with her mask dangling from her neck, breathing in great gulps of air. But the air wasn't fresh enough.

She should stay, she told herself, she should stay so that, in a little while, she could check on Manny. But her hands were removing the cap, mask, and gown, and her legs were carrying her away, beyond the operating room, past the recovery room, and even the waiting room. Those same legs started running up the stairs with the sure knowledge that the elevator would have been too slow.

When she reached the top landing, the sound of a second set of footsteps on the stairs registered, but that was all. The next thing she was aware of was that she was running through the parking lot. Where was her car? She'd have to calm down long enough to remember where she'd parked it.

Her arm was seized so hard and fast that she stumbled and would have fallen if Ariel hadn't also wrapped his free arm around her waist.

"Where the hell do you think you're going?"

Karen saw the anger in his eyes and felt it in his hard grip, but the commotion within her wouldn't allow her to feel anything beyond her own roiling emotions. "Away."

"No you aren't," he said in a low, forbidding voice. "Not until you tell me about Manny."

"He's fine."

"Then what's your problem, lady? Don't you like playing doctor anymore?"

"Playing?" She heard the hysteria in her voice and looked around wildly. People were turning their heads in her direction and she lowered her voice to a grating whisper. "I wouldn't call cutting into another person's body playing!"

"Neither would I." Ariel's features were tight. "But if you don't play at any other time, I figured you must be doing it in the office or at the hospital."

His sarcasm knifed into her, swift and sharp. "Just

because I won't play with you doesn't mean that I never have fun or that I don't know how to."

"When and where do you have fun?"

When? Where? The question hovered in her mind. When was the last time she'd had fun? Last week. With Ariel. With Ariel on a picnic. With Ariel on a cruiser. And before that? She couldn't remember.

"Well, Karen?"

She wanted to tell him that the only time in her whole life she'd experienced fun was with him, but her mouth refused to open. She stared at him, confused.

"You know what I think?" he asked quietly.

"No, Dr. Know-It-All, what do you think?"

His tan deepened with anger. "I think you want more than anything in the world to be a real woman, a woman called Karen. Only you don't know how. You think you only know how to be this person called Dr. Watts who's so brilliant and so powerful that Karen hasn't got a chance against her. I'm right, aren't I?"

"What do you care?"

Ariel pulled her up next to him, forcing her to walk alongside him. He said nothing and his silence was worse than his sarcasm. He hadn't said why he cared and Karen filled in the blank space with the only answer she could find. Ariel saw her as a challenge, one that he'd never encountered before: a woman who refused to fall for his charm.

"Get in."

He was holding a door open for her and she climbed in automatically, feeling like a robot who moved on command just as she'd always done. Be the best, her mother had ordered her, and she'd been the best. Marry a man with brains, her mother had told her, and she'd married Greg.

Her thoughts were like a carousel spinning out of

control. She was aware only of trying to regain self-possession, and when she discovered that Ariel had somehow maneuvered her into his car, she couldn't remember having climbed in. He was driving fast, much too fast, and she clutched at the side of the seat and dug her fingers into it.

"Stop it! You're going to kill us!"

He stopped so quickly that the back half of the car skidded on the sandy road. Karen flung her hands out in front of her, trying to break a fall she was sure was inevitable. But something stopped her body's movement. She looked down to see the seat belt and shoulder harness holding her back. Had she fastened it?

She looked over at Ariel, who was half-turned in the driver's seat, his left arm draped over the steering wheel, and his eyes probing her own once again. What was he looking for? What could he possibly hope to find? She was nothing more than a highly intelligent computer geared toward winning, toward success, wasn't she?

And then the tightly packed ball that was an accumulation of years of emotion began its inexorable rise. Her first encounter with Ariel, then the next when she'd hurt him, and finally the deep caring she'd felt for Manny's future had combined to set that ball spinning.

Following the operation, she'd had what was to her an aberrant thought: she'd succeeded again, she was too smart to lose, and she was sick of the winning when the cost was the loss of her personal vibrancy.

With the renewal of this thought, she searched for a vent, a receptacle for all the emotions converging on her simultaneously. Ariel had frightened her with his driving, perhaps on purpose. He would serve well as that vent.

"Who the hell do you think you are, forcing me into

your car and driving like a maniac! What do you want from me, you—you—" She sputtered in search of words that had always come so easily before.

Ariel opened the door, climbed out, and came around to open the passenger door. Reaching in, he released the seat belt and literally pulled Karen from the car.

She struggled to get her wrist loose from his hand, but it only hurt her skin. He was drawing her away from the car and down a hill steep enough that all she could do was try to keep her balance. And then he was leading her across a beach and down to the water, where the ocean seemed angry, the waves high and thunderous.

Ariel stopped and spoke words that she could hardly hear above the high-decibel beat of the ocean. "This is a good place to yell—go to it."

Karen was completely nonplussed. She wanted to do just what he'd suggested. She wanted to yell at him for daring to reach inside of her; to yell at herself for not daring to be a woman; even to yell at the ocean for moving in its natural rhythms.

But she didn't open her mouth. She shouted inside of herself, but none of it came out, only a question. "Where are we?" She could barely hear her own voice above the noise of the waves.

Ariel's eyes were an odd mixture of concern, laughter, and something unreachable. His words weren't so tiny as hers had been, his baritone cutting through the ocean's noise with more ease. "Don't you remember?" He pointed to a nearby spot. "That's where I built a fire and you ate too many hot dogs. That's also where I would have made love to you if the storm hadn't moved in so quickly from the sea."

Then he pointed up to the top of a sandy hill where his cottage sat. "And that's where I made a mistake."

One of his slow smiles began in his light-blue eyes and spread down to his mouth as if the smile was over-flowing.

Was he laughing at her? Because, if he were . . . "You think you're so smart."

"No," he said, "You're the one who thinks too many smart things." He laid all the emphasis on that one word—"smart." "If you're so smart, how come you deny half of what you are?"

"What makes you think you know everything?" she flung back at him.

"Just smart, I guess." His smile ballooned outward into laughter.

He *was* laughing at her. "Take me home!" Karen had forgotten his hand on her wrist, and as she took a step away, he jerked her back to him. "Let go of me this minute!"

"No." Instead, his grip tightened as he led her back up the hill, away from the thrashing waters. Yet Karen felt as if she carried much of the ocean's tumult right inside her. Briefly, she struggled against him once more as he opened his cottage door, but it was useless. He kicked the door closed and the sound of the big waves was gone. The blue-and-green living room was silent as Ariel released his hold and turned to face her. Looking down at her from his much greater height, he said, "Let me ask you some things about yourself."

"There's nothing you need to know about me."

Only the perpetual smile that was a natural phenomenon of his eyes remained. "Karen, why are you always so ready to explode right in my face? I haven't consciously tried to hurt you, not once since I've known you."

Karen used the age-old method of counting to ten and

was glad she had, for while she counted, she allowed her mind to glide over the times she'd been with Ariel.

"No, I suppose you haven't actually gone out of your way to anger me." There was a question, however, that had been lurking on the fringes. "What do you want from me? Yes, yes I know"—she gestured in dismissal of her own answer—"I was a challenge to you. But I'm sure that after last Saturday night you must have decided the hell with it."

Ariel backed up to one of the beanbag chairs and collapsed into it. "You're right," he said, looking up at her. "Come on, sit. All I want to do is talk to you." Once Karen sat down, he continued. "Like I said, you're right. The challenge was gone after the zingers you threw at me in the restaurant. All I wanted was to be alone. It was only some vague sense of manners that got me back to Susan and Jordan to tell them I'd leave my car for them. I fully intended on hitching a ride home. Only they rejected the idea and, in essence, me. They didn't need me or my car since they could walk from the restaurant to Jordan's place." He sighed and looked toward the small treasure chest sitting beneath the window. "I must admit, I haven't felt quite that lonely in a long time."

"Ariel, I . . ." What was she supposed to say? The truth?

"Don't tell me you're sorry. That's not what I want from you." Ariel struggled to sit up, but seemed to be trapped in the saggy, pellet-filled chair. "Dammit! Sometimes I feel like an octopus with these arms and legs going off on journeys without me."

Karen tried not to laugh, but he did resemble an octopus tangled up in green seaweed—figuratively anyway.

"Ariel," she said, the laughter still in her voice,

"how'd your legs get to be so long?" She looked at the offending appendages and then away. Why did she have such a thing for those legs? Men were supposed to look at *women's* legs, not the other way around.

"I was trying to grow fins but there was this genetic mixup when I was about fourteen. As I ate everything but the refrigerator shelves, my aunt claimed I was going to grow up to be a whale. My uncle, on the other hand, said that my voracious and indiscriminate appetite definitely indicated a great white shark." He chuckled. "Fooled 'em all. Grew up to be an octopus."

As Karen's smile faded, she wondered how Ariel could rise so easily from serious conversational depths to lighthearted joking. This simple musing turned into surprise when Ariel plunged right back down into the deep.

"But my tentacles are not the subject here." His clear-water eyes washed over her. "The subject is you. I got to thinking about you last night while I was reading about certain types of tropical fish."

A less-than-stunning analogy. "Are you calling me a fish?"

"Anything but. It was simply a characteristic of several species that sent me off dreaming about you." The chair released him and he stood and walked toward the window, where he continued his train of thought, his back to Karen. "What was it like in med school, being in the minority, being a woman in what is still mostly a man's world?"

Why was he asking her that? As off-the-wall as the question was, it was nevertheless an innocuous one, and she decided to answer. "It was like ... well, like being a square surrounded by triangles, and in order to appear the same, I had to cut myself in half and toss out the unnecessary side."

Ariel put his back to the window and stared at her. "An apt description. In other words, you had to play a role that, in a way, simulated masculinity?"

What was he driving at? "It wasn't all that hard. I'd been doing it for most of my life."

"Why?"

Questions, she wished he'd stop asking all these questions. "Because . . ." Oh, what was the difference? she thought in defeat. It didn't matter anyway. She'd already blown whatever chance she might have had to form a love relationship with this man. "Because that's the way my mother raised my sister and me. I don't know why, but my mother seemed to think that Liza was made for men and that I was made for books."

Ariel walked over to her and stretched his hand down to her. "Stand up for a minute."

"What for?"

"Just humor me." He helped her to her feet and then walked slowly around her, coming to a grinning halt in front of her. "You sure *look* like a woman."

Swiftly, Ariel bent his head, touching her lips with his while flicking out his tongue for the briefest taste before straightening back up. "You taste like a woman too."

Karen was confused, not so much by his action, but by her own reaction. She was angry at his presumption that he could simply kiss her whenever the mood struck him, but she was elated at his words and even more excited by his fleeting, erotic touch. Her confusion silenced her and so she stood, mutely staring up into the bluest eyes she'd ever seen.

Ariel's expression took on a faraway look. "Once, a long time ago, I knew someone who liked to play a fascinating game. This person called it 'roles.' One day when I was particularly depressed about my parents, we played the game. I took on the role of my father while my friend took on that of my mother. We must have played for a good hour, but when we were done, all my depression and anger were gone because of the insight I'd gained from pretending to be someone I wasn't. For the first time in my life, I understood why my father had done the things—all the things—he'd done."

"Why are you telling me this?"

"Because," Ariel said, "I like you. A lot. Because I trust you enough to tell you things that . . ." He looked away at nothing in particular and then back at Karen. "that I don't usually tell anyone."

Ariel felt reality drawing in on him, the reality of knowing what he planned to do next. He felt his insides tighten with the laughter that always came when there was something he didn't feel capable of facing, but he forced it back down. He could see how stiffly Karen stood there, how shallow her breath was. She was scared of something and he wanted to take away her fear. If he laughed, he'd never get the chance. It was just that the irony of it all had hit him unexpectedly. Here he was telling Karen he trusted her, about to ask her to trust him, when he suddenly wasn't too sure he even trusted himself.

Why was he doing this? Was it because he cared about this woman? How could he? He'd only met her a week and a half ago. Or was he looking for some sort of power? Maybe he'd never shaken the helpless feeling he'd had as a small child when his mother would leave him with her sister for the night. Maybe, unknown to himself, he believed he could wipe out that remembered helplessness by gaining power over this woman.

Then again, he could be duping himself completely. He could be telling himself he liked her so much and wanted to help her when, in reality, he was just trying to feed his ego by adding yet another woman to his list of the conquered. He didn't know, he just didn't know.

Ariel pulled back out of himself, focused on Karen once more, and thought of the scenario he'd been devising for this moment. It was crazy, but looking into her scared-doe eyes, he suddenly wanted to hand over all the power to her. He shook his head imperceptibly.

"Trust me," he said.

Chapter Five

He was crazy. Trust him? *She* was crazy, absolutely
loony, because that was exactly what she was preparing to do—trust him.

"Okay," Karen said. "You've got my trust . . . up to a
point." What if he asked her to define that point? Could
she?

Ariel took a single step closer. "Are you willing to
touch me?"

Good God. Touch him? She wanted to feel his golden
hair slip between her fingers and discover just how
much longer his legs were than hers by lying alongside
him. She wanted . . .

She licked her lips, an unconscious act that didn't go
unnoticed. "What do you mean—willing to touch you?"

Soft questions glistened from his light-blue eyes. "I'd
just feel better if we were sitting right next to each
other." He grinned boyishly. "I guess that, in some
ways, I'm like a three-year-old. I feel more confident
leaning against a grown-up woman."

Karen couldn't help smiling back at him. He was so
much a man, and yet he was also as ingenuous as the
three-year-old he'd mentioned. It was an irresistible
combination.

"All right," she said. "You can lean on me." She
laughed, feeling herself relax a little. "However, I could

topple over at any moment, and if you're leaning on me, you'll go down too."

Ariel chuckled. "Sounds fine to me."

He just stood there and Karen found herself wondering if he was quite as confident as he tried to appear. That small doubt mobilized her, gave her the sensation of having the upper hand, and she walked with more grace than usual to one of the beanbag chairs. After sinking down into it, she smiled up at Ariel, who was still rooted to the same spot. "Well?"

Ariel's feet came unstuck and in a split second Karen was rising as he displaced her with his greater weight in the chair.

As he pulled her closer to him, his body heat mixed rapidly with hers. She liked it and wanted more. He wore cutoffs and his right leg was stretched out, naked and strong, and she stretched out her left leg in a pretense of getting more comfortable. Their legs touched and she felt the wiry hairs on him. She shifted so their legs pressed closer together and she felt the tiniest pulse on the side of his knee.

"Karen?"

"Hmm?"

"Did you ever pretend things when you were a kid?"

"Sure."

"Give me some examples."

Karen turned her head to look at Ariel, discovered their faces were so close that she could see a tiny freckle just beneath the long lashes of his lower left eyelid. She wanted to ask him to close his eyes so she could kiss them. Instead, she looked away, afraid that he would say no, afraid he wouldn't like the way her lips felt on his skin.

He pulled his arm up from behind the chair and slid it carefully around her bare shoulders. "I used to pretend all the time. In one of my better fantasies I was Proteus, the ocean god, and like him, I could change my shape at will."

Karen's concentration was on the way Ariel's hand molded to her shoulder. She kept expecting him to move it, to slide his palm sensually along her arm, but he didn't. Her trust grew a little stronger.

"And what shapes . . ." She cleared her throat, trying to get rid of the peculiar squeek in her voice. "What shapes did you take on?"

"Fierce, powerful things. Killer whales and great white sharks and . . ." He laughed. "Gee, I seem to remember being a moray eel more than once. Ugly things, those eels."

Still his hand didn't move and she found herself thinking about it less. She knew she was relaxing and she knew it was because of Ariel's easy manner, his lazy tone of voice, his lounging body.

Ariel resisted the impulse to slide his hand along her arm—so smooth, so warm. How can I do this? he wondered. Hell! Here I am trying to calm her down when Ariel Singer the Great is preparing to leap out of his skin at the least provocation. If an ant coughs, I'm done for.

"Your turn, Karen. What did you used to pretend?" Maybe she'd give him some clue on how to begin.

Dammit, but she felt good, so close and warm like this. If only he could dispense with all the pretend stuff and just take a taste. No, a stupendous, monumental, absolutely monstrous bite. He pictured himself as an enormous shark, jaws wide, racing hell-bent-for-leather after a petite minnow. Before he could catch it, the laughter was tumbling out of him.

His laughter startled her. Nothing funny had happened, as far as she could see. Was he laughing at her?

Karen stiffened and leaned away from Ariel. "What are you laughing at?"

"Me. For a second there, my mind took off without me."

Karen looked at him again, then relaxed when she realized that, whatever had made him laugh, it was his own doing, not hers.

After musing over it for a short time, she remembered her favorite childhood fantasy. An odd one, now that she thought about it.

"I used to pretend that I was living in Colonial times and that I was captured by these absolutely savage Indians, only they were kind to me and taught me how to be just like them. Instead of having to do my arithmetic lessons, I learned how to skin a deer and roast it. And instead of politely sitting at a table eating dinner with a fork in my hand and a napkin in my lap, I could rip off great chunks of meat and eat with my hands while sitting cross-legged in the grass."

Had she said too much? Ariel's eyes were sparkling.

"How old were you," he asked slowly, "when you stopped pretending?"

Why did she feel she had to answer his question with great care? "I really don't know. Anyway, I wasn't doing it when I was seventeen."

"Are you sure?"

"Of course I'm sure." Was she? "Seventeen-year-olds don't pretend like that." Did they?

Ariel's hand tightened a fraction on her shoulder. "I *still* pretend. It's fun. Besides, like I was telling you, it can be therapeutic." He was quiet for the span of two breaths. "How about it, Karen? So far, your day has been pretty tough. I know your apparent dislike for games, but wouldn't it be nice to stop being the successful woman doctor for a little while and go back to some of that freedom you had when you were a kid?"

Karen sighed. She couldn't remember ever having had freedom when she was a kid. Maybe it would be fun to find out what it was she had missed.

"Okay. But if you're talking about playing roles, you'll have to teach me. I've never done it before."

Ariel gave her shoulder an affectionate squeeze. "Sure you have. You used to play the role of a white girl captured by the wild Indians."

Karen's eyebrows shot up. "You don't mean—"

"Yes, I do. Why not? Can I be the Indian? If I can't be the Indian, I don't wanna come over to your house no more." He grinned. "Won't let you come to my house no more neither."

He'd caught her with the fun in his eyes. And, yes, it *had* been a tough day—maybe even a tough lifetime in some ways.

"All right, Ariel. You can be the Indian."

Ariel stood, then reached out his hand to help her up. He pointed to the kitchen area. "That's where you live with your mother and father. He's a schoolmaster and she's"—he glanced away, then back again—"a tired, bitter housewife with too many children."

He swept his arm, indicating the small living room. "This is a field just outside your village where you like to go and play even though you've been forbidden to do so."

Then he pointed to the bedroom. "That's where the Indians are. It's not a permanent village, just a place where the braves are camped, getting ready to raid your settlement."

Karen hesitated. "I don't know what I'm supposed to do."

"Just follow my lead and let the game take over. It will, I promise."

Karen wasn't so sure, but she surprised herself with the overwhelming desire to be a good sport. She turned away from Ariel, walked into the kitchen, looked around uncertainly, then sat down at the small table. When she glanced back toward the living room, Ariel was no longer there.

It was quiet, *awfully* quiet. She drummed her fingers on the table. What was he doing? A minute went by. Then another. She kicked off her sandals and wiggled her hot toes. Now that she thought of it, this was exactly the way the childhood fantasy used to work. She'd pretend for long minutes that she was in her rustic home, sitting at a table doing her lessons. Then, while her mother was busy doing the gardening or churning butter, she'd see her chance and sneak out of the house.

Karen stood up, pretending that her mother was momentarily out of sight. She could almost hear the rhythmic clunking of the butter churn. The sound faded as she slipped out the door, down the packed-dirt lane, and out into the field.

Her heart was pounding, the child's heart, Karen's heart. Quietly, she rounded the corner of the counter separating the kitchen from the living room. She pretended the counter was a farmer's fieldstone wall. So quiet. So very . . .

Arms slammed around her legs and she almost screamed as she pitched backward. The arms caught her just before she would have hit the floor.

"Mine!" he exclaimed. "You fall in trap of great warrior and now you mine."

Something happened in her mind, something went *snap!* and it was like she was a child again when the fantasy could be as real as life itself. She struggled, but the Indian was big and strong, and the more she struggled, the tighter he held her.

Her heart's tempo doubled, and suddenly, looking into clear-water eyes, she saw herself, not as a child, but as a teenager lying in her dark bed, pretending she'd just been captured by a savage Indian. He was going to force her to do what good girls weren't supposed to do, but it was okay, no one could blame her because it wouldn't be her fault.

Ariel saw the look, the one in her eyes that said yes. He'd guessed right. Nicole had once told him that there were a lot of women who had a hard time accepting the responsibility for their own desires. For too many years, they'd been taught that "good girls don't." He'd been right to think that Karen had extended her Indian fantasy right up through her teens.

He was afraid to break any spell he might have woven, but it was now or never.

"Karen?"

"Yes?"

"I want to make love to you."

His heart pounded painfully in his chest as he waited. What was she thinking? Why wasn't she answering?

Karen felt how strong his arms were around her, felt his long thighs pressed against her back as he held her, saw the overpowering need in his eyes.

She swallowed. "Then do it. Make love to me."

Still holding her up with his legs and one arm, he raised his hand to brush his palm down her flushed cheek.

"Soft." His voice was low, quiet. He slid his hand along her neck, over her shoulder, and down to the tender skin inside her elbow where he lightly traced a circle and sent a tremor throughout her warming body.

"Sensitive." He lifted her arm to his lips and ran his tongue along the same spot on her arm.

Only half-aware of what was happening, Karen allowed Ariel to pull her up onto her feet and lead her into the bedroom. She had an insane desire to rip off her clothes—his, too—and leap onto the bed. She grinned.

Ariel tilted his head to the side. "And what makes this lady so happy?"

Should she tell him? "I want this. I mean I really *want* this."

"Me too."

And then they were standing face-to-face with only enough room left between them for removing their clothes while they watched, not themselves, but each other.

When Ariel stepped out of his cutoffs, Karen's fingers froze at the shoulder strap of her bra. Well for . . . He doesn't wear those terrible Jockey shorts. She smiled at what she saw. Matter of fact, he doesn't wear a single, solitary thing!

Their clothing lay scattered on the floor as, together, they sank down onto the bed.

"Touch me, Karen. Touch me and let me tell you how it makes me feel."

At first, her fingers trembled as she lifted her hand to his sun-colored hair, but the trembling stopped as she felt the soft strands slide pleasantly through her fingers.

"Like the currents," he whispered. "Like the currents deep in the ocean pulling me deeper still." And when she leaned over him and touched her lips to his chest, he said, "It makes my heart pound, makes me want to dive down even farther."

Karen felt as if something were growing within her. Was it her own need to explore the depths? Yes, that and a certain new confidence in herself as a woman. He liked her touch, he responded to it.

His hands started touching her wherever she touched him: her lips, her breasts, her stomach, her thighs. And he talked softly all along, telling her how she made him feel. Karen felt what he felt. Her heart pounded like the breakers he described and her skin tingled with the heat of the tropical waters he told her about and, oh, how she wanted more and more and . . .

And he was inside, outside. He was everywhere, and the waves came faster and still he talked to her, a low murmur in her ear telling her what he felt. It was hot noon in the tropics and his voice was the panting wind and it was so unbearably hot, and she had to, she just couldn't help it, she *had* to be released from this searing pressure. It was then that all the hot waters seemed to swell and curl and then crash over and through her in great waves of relief.

As the last wave sighed away, neither of them moved neither of them spoke as each descended from the heights.

She'd enjoyed it. She'd actually enjoyed it! She'd given him pleasure and he'd given it back. Karen lay very still, feeling Ariel's body heavy on hers. Then slowly, like a creeping predator, came a thought.

He tricked me. He knew what he was going to do right along. He had it planned from the beginning. I challenged him. It was a game. My God, it was just a game!

She needed an excuse. "Oh, for heaven's sake, Ariel, I forgot Manny! How could I *do* that?" She pushed Ariel off her, rolled away, slid off the bed, and grabbing her clothes, dressed faster than she could ever remember having done before. The air felt cold on skin that was still damp from love in the afternoon, and she tried desperately to ignore the fingers of ecstasy still playing with every nerve in her body.

Ariel lay there stunned. What had happened? She'd found as much pleasure in their lovemaking as he had. There was no mistaking *that*. Then what was wrong? Had he hurt her somehow?

"Karen, what did I do?"

"Nothing."

He sat up, feeling exposed far beyond his nudity. "Then why are you mad at me?"

"I'm not." She was dressed and standing with her back to him.

"Turn around, Karen. Look at me." When she wouldn't, Ariel got up, walked over, and planted himself in front of her. "Look at me."

When she finally raised her eyes, he saw it. She was hurting inside. And that touch of coldness he saw, where had it come from?

Her eyes narrowed. "I think I've just been had."

Ariel grinned nervously. And his nerves made him say the first thing that came into his mind. "You're right. You've been had. And I'd like to have you again and again and again."

"Forget it!" she shouted at him. "I've decided I really don't like games after all!"

A curse escaped him before he could catch it. It stunned him, but then he thought, well, who cares anyway! An inordinately contrary voice answered, I care. He ignored the voice. Why the devil should he care? She was just another woman, and she was a damned strange one at that. He didn't care at all. Yes, you do, whispered the little voice.

He whipped his cutoffs up off the floor, jammed his

foot in, got his toe tangled in a thread, swore, pushed until the thread broke with a popping sound—which hurt his toe—swore again, then finished dressing without incident.

He eyed her rigid back and sighed inwardly at the thought of how pliant it had been such a short time ago. "I guess I better take you back to the hospital," he said softly.

Without looking at him, Karen walked swiftly out of the bedroom. "I guess you better."

Relieved to find Fran's note on the typewriter saying that she'd gone home, Karen had immediately gone to the shower, hoping to wash away the events of the day. But the streaming water and the lathery soap could do nothing more than remove the heady aroma of Ariel's body. When she stepped out of the shower to dry herself, she realized she was sorry to have erased the tantalizing fragrance. She pushed away the thought with an abrasive toweling and then flung on her jeans and sweatshirt. She'd decided to go where the brisk air might halt the flowing memories.

The beach was almost deserted because of a bleakness that could only be found on such a cloudy day by the ocean. Just one other person was in view, and that was a man much farther down the beach surf casting. She watched for a few minutes as he drew back his rod and then flicked it forward, expertly sending his line out beyond the dirt-colored breakers.

Karen turned away and walked in the opposite direction with the damp ocean wind whipping her hair around her face. Then she stopped to face the wind, the ocean, the calling gulls—things wise to their own nature.

"What have I done?" she whispered to the gray waters. Resolutely, she pushed away the answer and thought instead of Manny, of how he'd be released the next day, since he was doing fine. And then she thought of how she'd have to go to the hospital in the morning and she wondered if Ariel would be there to bring Manny home.

Karen looked far out across the ocean but could find none of the serenity that others claimed to find by the sea. The rhythm of the small waves slapping the wet sand carried her thoughts back to Ariel's small cottage.

She should have been glad—ecstatic really—to find that she was far from an unresponsive woman. But Karen was unnerved and angry after going over the specifics of Ariel's lovemaking. He'd almost done it once during an approaching storm, and this time, he had. She realized that his foreplay had been not so much a toying with her body as it was a game he'd played with her mind. What had he done physically?

A wave slid up the gentle rise of sand and licked briefly at her sneakered foot before racing back to its source. With his hand, he'd touched her cheek, her arm, her breasts, her stomach, and even the nucleus of her body—but he'd done so only for a moment. And with his tongue he'd tasted her mouth, her ear, and again, that nucleus. But each touch had been nothing more than a fleeting caress.

Images of making love with Greg tumbled into her mind like the waves on the shore. There had been times when he'd taken an hour or more with foreplay, kissing her, touching her in many more places than Ariel had. But nothing greater than tiny bits of arousal had glimmered through her. How was it that Ariel had only to talk to her? Greg had always held a determined silence. Karen laughed into the wind. Ariel had said that all he had wanted to do was to talk to her. And that's exactly what he'd done.

That was Wednesday, a day of success in the operating room, and a different sort of success also—success in physical love.

Thursday was filled with neither success nor failure; rather, it was a day replete with myopia, dirt in eyes, glaucoma, and the myriad other visual ailments to which humans are prone. But Thursday also contained Karen's own brand of diseased eyesight: no matter what she did, no matter where she looked, she saw Ariel in her mind's eye. She knew she was struggling within herself, that there was something she should really be facing right now, but it wasn't until Friday morning, when she woke up after a sensationally weird dream, that she realized she could no longer avoid emotional reality.

Karen lay in bed staring at the ceiling where the dream images played across the plain white background. She could still see her dream self standing and peering into a distorted mirror. The reflections shifted in form from one person to another, yet she knew that each was a version of herself. First, she was her mother in the mirror and then mother-Karen drifted into being Liza-Karen. But the most disturbing reflection had been the one in which Karen had seen herself standing there wearing a man's suit with her shoulder-length hair cut off into a man's style. Karen's masculine image broke up like a puzzle dropped on the floor and then came back together again wearing different clothes and long, flowing hair. The clothes were made of leather, both tough and soft like an Indian might wear. The mirror's image dissolved, and in its place stood Ariel. The final portion of the dream was auditory. She heard herself saying to him, "If I learn to be like leather, both tough and soft, will I be complete? Will you love me the way I love you?"

Karen closed her eyes, trying to shut out the images and the words, but she couldn't. Was it really possible? Could she be in love with a man she'd known for two weeks? Yes, it had to be possible because that was exactly what had happened.

"Ariel," she whispered to the room, "I love you." She flipped over onto her stomach, burying her face in the pillow, and her words were a muffled cry to the emptiness around her. "But you don't love me back."

The rest of the day took on the tone of her mood. Only when she was peering through the ophthalmoscope, where she could immerse herself in the ever-amazing structure of the human eye, did she forget that she was aching inside. Karen was glad that her practice had built to the point where almost every minute was filled with someone else's problems.

At eight o'clock in the evening when the telephone rang, she was startled out of another morbid reverie.

"Karen," Susan's voice was almost a whisper, "I just had to talk with you."

"Is something the matter?" Could anyone have worse troubles than her own?

"Yes, it's Jordan. He left a few hours ago because I blew up at him."

Susan never got mad. What could Jordan have possibly done? "Why'd you do that?"

"Because he's leaving for the Bahamas tomorrow morning, and as he put it, he wanted me in bed with him one last time." Susan's sigh was an audible hiss over the phone. "He didn't say he loved me or that he would miss me, and he didn't ask me to see him off in the morning. All he wanted was one last fling."

Karen thought about Jordan's genuine concern the

day they'd all gone fishing. He'd said that Susan couldn't be just another woman in another port for him.

"Susan, I think you misinterpreted. Don't you remember what I told you Jordan had said to me the day we went fishing? He loves you, I know he does. Give him time. He'll be back."

"Not after what I said to him." Susan's voice hinted of tears.

"What did you say?"

Susan sniffed. "I told him he was a freeloader in more than just the usual sense. I said that he not only used us to provide himself with the comforts of home when he and Ari were in college, but that he was now trying to provide himself with a sexual diversion in this area."

"Oh for God's sake, Susan, why did you have to go and say a thing like that?"

Now it was obvious that Susan was crying. "Because I . . . I don't want to . . . be without him anymore."

"You have a hell of a way of showing it!" Calm down, she told herself. Susan needs your help, not your derision. "Can you catch up with him? Do you know where he went?"

Karen could hear Susan blowing her nose. "I called his apartment but there was no answer, so I figured he might be with Ariel, but there was no answer at his place either. I don't know what to do."

Neither did Karen. "What can I do to help?"

"I don't know—just letting me cry on the phone has helped a little. Listen, I'm going to hang up and try to reach either Jordan or Ariel again. Maybe, if I keep trying, I'll find him."

"Wait a minute," Karen said. "Don't hang up. Tell me first what you refused to tell me last Saturday. You said something about having it all figured out as if you knew of some way to be with Jordan wherever he went."

"Yeah, I thought I had it all figured out. All I needed was Jordan to tell me that he loved me enough to want me with him all the time. You see, I went into residency for ear, nose, and throat because I thought I had to specialize in something. Everyone else did. What I really wanted to do was sort of specialize in everything. I used to have dreams of being an old-time country doctor. But who does that these days? Anyway, Jordan goes out on a lot of long-term expeditions and, often enough, the people involved need a doctor. I thought I could learn some of the special techniques needed for dealing with ocean injuries and become, well, what would you call it? A ship's doctor, I guess."

Karen grinned. "But that's marvelous! Oh, Susan, you've got to get a hold of him. Now you can hang up." She paused. "One more thing."

"What's that?"

"Good luck."

Karen walked away from the telephone with the smile still on her face. It would work out, she just knew it would. Two people in love like that were not supposed to spend their lives apart.

She was about to head upstairs when the doorbell rang. Karen's first thought was that it might be Ariel. But then she realized that he and Jordan were probably off somewhere together. She opened the door more out of curiosity than any desire to talk with anyone. Jordan was the last person she expected to see shifting from one foot to the other on her doorstep like a dog with cold feet.

"May I come in?"

She swung the door wide. "Of course." She peered around behind him. "Are you alone?"

Jordan laughed. "Yeah. I didn't want Ariel with me. He's got the worst case of cranks I think I've ever seen.

All he does is glower and grunt. I've got enough on my mind without having to listen to his crocodile noises."

Karen closed the door and sat down on the couch while Jordan plopped down in a chair. His face wrinkled into a frown, making Karen laugh. "You look rather like a crocodile yourself."

Jordan grunted, smiled briefly, and once again grew serious. "The best way to say what I've got to say is to just say it. Hell! What goes through the minds of women?"

"Depends," Karen said, "on what woman you're talking about." She knew he was referring to Susan, but she wasn't sure yet whether she should let on that she'd already spoken with her friend. It would be best to find out first what Jordan wanted to talk about.

"I mean Susan. I was up in Boston with her a while ago and she got madder than I've ever seen her before. She all but kicked me out of her apartment. And you want to know why? Well, you're going to know, because I'm going to tell you. She got mad because I wanted to make love to her."

"Jordan, is that what you *really* wanted to do? Make love to her?"

Jordan cocked his head to the side and Karen was once again reminded of a dog, this time a confused puppy, a rather large one. Then his jaw dropped open and snapped closed again. "You don't mean—? Yes, you do. Are you asking me if I wanted to take Susan to bed because I love her or because it just seemed like the best idea at the moment?"

"Precisely."

Jordan wiped his hand across his face in a troubled gesture. "Oh, dear Lord. I love her, Karen. I love her so much that I've even been thinking of giving up my career and going into a more sedentary branch of oceanography."

Karen thought her face must be splitting in half with her grin. "Good, but you don't have to. Susan will give up hers instead. All you have to do is say the word."

"What in blue blazes are you talking about, woman?"

"I'm talking about the fact that you love Susan and Susan loves you back. She doesn't, however, love ears, noses, and throats exclusively."

"Huh?"

Karen felt sure that Susan would forgive her for divulging the contents of their telephone conversation, and so she told Jordan of Susan's dream of being a ship's doctor. When she'd finished, he sat there looking slightly dazed. Karen waited patiently for him to digest what she'd told him before asking, "What are you going to do about it?"

"I think," he said slowly, "that I'm going to climb in my car and drive back up to Boston." He stood up. "Thanks, Karen."

"Just a minute." Should she? It was too late to weigh the pros and cons; her mouth was already forming the question. "Where's Ariel?"

"Over at the MBL. Why?"

"Just curious," she lied.

Jordan folded his arms and looked down at her. "He's an interesting character, isn't he?"

"Yes."

"Only problem is, Karen, you can't figure out where he's coming from, can you?"

That was an understatement. She gave a humorless laugh. "He seems at times to be coming from all directions and then, at others, to be flying away."

"I wish I could help you, but I can't. To tell you the truth, Ariel hasn't talked about you to me at all. Nothing. And right at this moment, he's not talking to anyone about anything. He's sitting in the library at the

MBL glaring at some pictures of tropical fish called indigo hamlets." Jordan shook his head. "I think Ariel's finally gone completely bananas."

For the rest of the evening, Karen sat alternately staring at a journal of ophthalmology and at nothing whatsoever. She kept hoping to hear the phone ring, to hear Susan's voice saying that everything had worked out after all. But the phone didn't ring, not until she'd climbed into bed.

She lifted the receiver, breathless from having run down the stairs and into the kitchen. "Hello?"

"Hi." It was Ariel. "What are you doing?"

"Standing in the kitchen listening to you ask me what I'm doing."

"What were you doing before I called?"

Trying not to think about you. "Trying to sleep."

Pause. "Did I wake you up?"

"No."

Another pause. "Why not?"

Karen laughed in exasperation. "Ariel, what did you call about?"

"I'm not sure. The phone was here and so was I. It just seemed natural to pick it up and use it."

"Has anyone ever told you you're a little strange?"

His laugh had a soft, breathy quality. "Yeah, lots of times. Would you mind spending a bit more time with a maniac?"

Mind? She'd sell her soul for the chance. "What did you have in mind?"

"Nothing. It just dawned on me."

"Ariel, will you please straighten up?"

For a moment, she thought he'd hung up after she heard a clatter and then silence. Was he drunk? Then he came back on the line. "Okay, I straightened up. Place wasn't much of a mess anyway."

"Have you been drinking?"

"Nope. Do I sound it?"

"Yes," Karen answered emphatically, "you do."

"The MBL does strange things to my head. I just got back from there. You do strange things to my head too." Now there was an almost interminable pause. "Karen . . . I want to make love to you all over again."

"Is *that* why you're calling?"

"I think so . . . yes, that's why I'm calling."

As much as she wanted precisely the same thing, Karen knew she couldn't just say yes. She couldn't have him thinking that all he had to do was call her up anytime and have her come running. And as well as his Indian fantasy had worked, something about it was bothering her. "I'm not at your beck and call."

"I'm at yours."

Karen laughed, more in self-derision than at anything else. "I didn't know that savages would allow their captives any say in what, when, or how."

"Want to switch?"

What was this man thinking about? "Ariel, what are you saying?"

"I'm saying that I'll let you be a man if you want."

"I don't want to be a man."

"I don't mean permanently." His breathing was almost a tangible thing in her ear. "I mean, just pretend."

"I don't want to pretend either."

"Why not? That's what you've been doing for most of your life, isn't it? Why not complete the picture for yourself? Really act it out?"

Karen took a deep breath, but the anger and hostility his words set brewing within her wouldn't dissipate. "I don't need this. I don't need you or anyone else trying to make fun of the way in which I've led my life. I don't need *you.*" She slammed down the receiver.

Karen stomped up the stairs, threw herself down on the bed, and pounded her fist into the pillow. "Damn him!" Then she burst into tears. It was dawn before she fell asleep.

At ten o'clock Saturday morning, the telephone's persistent ringing woke her up. It was Susan calling to tell her what she already knew: Jordan had asked her to marry him. It was a long conversation filled mostly with Susan's voice going on and on about all her plans for the future.

Karen swung the mouthpiece away long enough to yawn widely. She'd never felt quite this tired. "Have you set the date?"

"No, we're both being vague about it since I have to take some time to close down my practice and Jordan has a job down in the Bahamas. He's not sure how long it'll last. Could be a few days or weeks or months. He just doesn't know."

Karen remembered her own outsized wedding when she'd married Greg. "Are you planning a big wedding?"

Susan laughed. "No, I couldn't do that to Jordan. I think he'd suffocate in a tux. We'll just do it quietly without bothering a soul."

Karen envisioned Susan's future. "Before you know it, you're going to be leading a life full of adventure."

For the next four days, Karen found herself envying Susan, wishing that she, too, could have love-filled adventures to look forward to. All she had was her practice, her lonely house, and perhaps the eerie beauty of the coastal winter to come. There was only one thing wrong with that life: it was empty of Ariel.

By Thursday, Karen had used harsh, cold thoughts to inoculate herself against her sad infection. When, at

four-thirty in the afternoon, she smiled a farewell to
Fran for the day, she gave herself a mental pat on the
back.

"Well, smart lady," she said aloud to the coral walls
of the waiting room, "you've licked your wounds clean
and you've healed yourself right back to good as new.
The hell with Ariel!"

She walked toward the door to lock it when it opened
and Ariel stepped in. "You wouldn't lock out a patient,
would you?"

Karen stood in stunned silence. What was he doing
here, looking his normal, ramshackle, handsome self
complete with snug jeans—ripped in the thigh—and
T-shirt stretched across his broad chest?

"Well, would you?"

"Would I what?" She was confused all over again.
Hadn't she hung up on him? Wasn't he upset about
that? Wasn't *she* upset?

"Would you lock out a patient?" His eyes smiled at
her with mischief, even though, as usual, his mouth
remained passive.

She put her hand to her chest in an unconscious gesture. Her heart was pounding as if it might break
through her ribs. "You're not a patient."

"Yes I am. I need therapy. I need another picnic with
a beautiful lady doctor whose heavenly eyes can wash
away my sins."

Her mind was filled with gibberish and her tongue
reacted instantly to it. "Why are you here? I mean,
where've you been? I mean . . . Oh, I don't know what I
mean."

"Miss me?"

"Yes." Try again. "No." That wasn't true. "Maybe."
Phooey!

Ariel stepped in and shut the door behind him.

"Karen, you're making just about as much sense as an upside-down tulip." His warm palms closed on her cool cheeks. "I've been finishing up a job for an oil company. They're thinking of drilling off the coast here and they hired me to study the possible effects."

Captured between his hands, she had nowhere to look but at Ariel. What was that line high up on his left cheekbone? A scratch? "How did you cut yourself?"

"A clam bit me."

"Oh, come on. Clams don't bite." How was she managing to speak with such lightness when her body was feeling so heavy, so drugged? She wanted to touch his injured skin, to kiss it and make the hurt go away. But it was only in her mind that she reached out to him; her hands simply fluttered at her sides like dry leaves in the wind.

"The hell with my face. I'd rather talk about yours, which looks in need of food." He dropped his hands and turned to lock the door. "Let's go," he said, grabbing her hand and pulling her into the hall that led toward the private part of her house.

Why wasn't she telling him to leave? Because he was confusing her, that's why. "Where are we going?"

He was slightly ahead of her, leading her through the living room and to the bottom of the stairs. With a tug, he forced her to lift her foot onto the first step. "Go change into a bathing suit and throw some old clothes on over it." When she hesitated, he said, "You don't want me to do it for you . . . we'd never get out of here."

That mobilized her. Yet, as she exchanged her simple dress for the clothing he'd specified, she wondered why it had. Karen had known for almost a week now that she loved him and that, more than anything, she wanted to have him blend his body with hers. Why had it frightened her that he might follow her up to her bedroom? Then she remembered the late-night phone conversation with him. He'd angered her. And his hint at switching sexual roles had given her a terrible bout of anxiety.

Then why wasn't she refusing to go out with him now? Because she couldn't help herself. Karen wanted to be with him at all costs, even if the price was the destruction of the intellectual wall she'd so carefully built around her over the years.

The BMW sped down the familiar road leading to Centerville and then onto the smaller road that soon brought them to a halt beside Ariel's isolated cottage overlooking the Atlantic.

Karen had been silent during the drive while Ariel had talked pleasantly and impersonally about his recently completed project. She heard very little of what he said, since most of her thoughts had been busily trying to unravel themselves.

He was opening the door for her before she was fully aware that they had stopped. "Strip to your bathing suit. The tide's up, the waves are down, and we can make like a couple of fish before we eat some of the same."

Karen stepped out alongside Ariel and turned to look at the ocean. He might think the waves were down, but they seemed pretty high to her. "I can't swim."

Chapter Six

❧

Karen had often chided herself for not learning to swim better, and now she stood in utter embarrassment before a man who spent much of his life near, on, and under the water. Quickly, she corrected herself. "I mean, I *can* swim, but really only enough to keep myself alive."

As Ariel smiled at her, Karen realized he had dimples—no, not dimples, twin creases on each side of his mouth that deepened when his smile widened. Why hadn't she noticed that before?

He took her hand and squeezed it. "I'll stay with you and hold you the whole time. I won't let you get hurt."

Karen glanced back down to where the waves arched their liquid backs before springing on their prey of soft beige sand. It looked dangerous to her, and yet this man who held her hand knew that water and knew her too. His knowledge and her new love for him combined to make her want to place her life in his hands. She looked up at him. "I know you won't let me get hurt. Besides"—she smiled a touch sheepishly—"how can I continue living on the Cape without swimming in the ocean?"

"Or," he said, holding her eyes with his own, "dating an oceanographer without getting wet?"

Dating? Is that what he considered this? A date? She

waited outside while he went into the cottage to change. Slipping out of her jeans and blouse, she wondered again, as she had often in the past four days, what Ariel thought of her. She had decided that he considered her a friend, and when he'd invited her out here this afternoon, she'd been sure he'd done so because of that friendship. If he'd desired her company as a woman, wouldn't he have called her, or come to see her before now? But he'd said she was "dating" him. Friends *went* places together; they didn't date each other.

When Ariel came back wearing only a pair of very short cutoff jeans and two towels draped around his neck, Karen felt an immediate arousal. His legs were the source of all his height and she couldn't tear her eyes away from their tautly muscled length.

Even when he stopped in front of her, her eyes still slid along the tanned skin of his legs.

"I'm sorry, Karen, but I won't allow you to consume my legs. I need them for swimming." He drew her face up with a finger beneath her chin. "Afterward, however, I might let you take a nibble."

Yes, she thought, that's just what she'd like to do. But not a nibble. She'd like to taste each one, she'd like to run her tongue along the tender insides of his thigh right up to . . . What was the *matter* with her? She had the absurd notion that her thoughts were so vivid as to be audible.

His eyes held a mixture of delight and sensuality. "Whatever you were just thinking must have been an exquisite idea. Share it with me . . . later." He put his arm around her and turned her toward the beach. "For now, this lady needs some cool waters."

He could say *that* again, she thought as they descended the small, steep hill to the beach.

The cold water slapping at her legs washed away her hot thoughts and she clung to Ariel's hand as he walked her out until the salty sea came up to her chest. Sudden, irrational fears crept into her mind.

"What's out here in this water? Are there any sharks or squishy stinging things?" She waited for him to laugh at her, but he didn't.

"Sharks aren't in the habit of vacationing on the shores of Cape Cod, and they usually prefer fish to people. As for squishy things, well, let's see . . . There's the occasional *Cyanea capillata*, or in hurricane season, a *Physalia physalis* might be driven ashore." He grinned at her and, once again, she noted the deep double creases like quote marks on either side of his mouth. "When you get right down to it, your greatest danger at this moment is from a certain *Homo sapiens*, male gender."

Karen had to laugh. "Do marine biologists always speak in Latin?"

"Only when necessary."

Karen found that her swimming ability was amplified by the heavier salt water, and soon she was truly enjoying herself. Feeling more confident, she told Ariel that, if he wanted to, he could move away from her so that he could swim more freely. She swam closer to shore, where she could feel the sand beneath her feet, and then turned to watch him. She was gently rocked by the swells of water, but she ignored their smooth sensuality in favor of the spectacle before her.

Ariel swam with the natural elegance of a dolphin. He didn't fight the water but stroked it and, at times, it seemed to return his caress. Karen thought she might happily watch this god of the sea forever, but soon he came in closer to her, disappeared beneath the surface, and then shot up, his body arching so that he sliced back down into the water like a knife through soft butter. This, she found, was where all her pleasure lay—not in her own swimming, but in watching the strength and grace with which Ariel became one with the ocean.

He broke the surface again right next to her and stood up, his hair darkened by the streaming water, his lush fringe of eyelashes adhering to themselves like spears glittering in the sunshine. She felt her heart expand as she looked up at him. His lips were so close that, if he'd leaned down but a fraction, he could have pressed his mouth to hers. He didn't. Instead, he wrapped his arm around her slender waist and turned her toward the beach. "I don't know about you, sweet woman, but if I don't eat soon, even the sharks won't want me."

Karen helped him build a fire before they brought supplies and food down from the cottage, including butter, lemon, and fresh corn on the cob. They sat companionably shucking the corn, buttering it, and wrapping it in foil.

Standing and starting up the hill, Ariel said, "Be back in a minute."

"Where are you going?"

"Have to get the main course."

She watched him go back up to the car, take out a large white carton with a metal handle, and then carry it back down, setting it on a nearby rock. She eyed it and Ariel's squatting figure suspiciously. "What's that?"

"*Homarus americanus*," he said without looking at her.

"Ariel," she said, "speak English."

"Lobster."

Karen giggled and then stopped as she thought how

appalling it was for a thirty-year-old to giggle like a teenager. "Good. I've always liked those red creatures."

"They're not red."

"What do you mean?"

"Come on over and take a look."

Seconds later, she was straightening up and backing away. "They're not dead!"

Ariel dropped to his knees and looked up at her with narrowed eyes. "You've never cooked a lobster?"

"I've only eaten them."

He looked down at the box and shoved an escaping lobster back in. "Uh, Karen, why don't you get the corn into the coals while I do some necessary dissections?"

"Are you going to kill them?"

He tilted his head around to her. "You're not in the habit of eating meat while it's still alive, are you?"

Karen swung around and put all her attention into the business of cooking corn. She glanced once at Ariel, saw a sharp knife in his hand, and quickly looked away. How could he cut into a living thing? Then she thought of a cataract operation she'd performed more than a year ago. She'd been cutting into live tissue then. But that was different. She hadn't murdered the patient. That word "murder" stayed in her mind as she watched Ariel place the two lobsters, now dead and split lengthwise, on the grill.

"Ariel, how could you?" She swallowed hard as he calmly basted them with butter. "You murdered them in cold blood!"

"No," he said, sitting back in the sand and looking directly at her. "I killed them. There's a difference."

"I see no difference."

"Karen, what did you have for dinner last night?"

She thought back to the night before. Had she eaten? Yes. "Lamb chops."

Ariel's eyes held gentle accusation. "Where did they come from?"

"The supermarket."

He grinned at her. "Come on, lady, you can do better than that."

Now she realized what he was getting at. "But that's not the same."

"Isn't it? Someone must have killed that soft little sheep baby so you could sink your teeth into it and lick your lips afterward."

Karen frowned. "You're being obscene."

"No," he said, "I'm being honest. We're meat-eating animals, but we've separated ourselves so much from the basics of our bodies, denying them with our so-called higher civilization, that we can actually pick up a slab of muscle in the market and call it meat without visualizing the steer with its soft brown eyes or the duck floating on a pond with the sun warming its feathered body." He gave her a smile of pure innocence. "End of lecture."

Karen's anger dissolved and she smiled back at him. "You're right."

As they began eating what turned out to be a delectable meal, Karen considered Ariel's use of the Latin names for ocean creatures. "By the way, would you translate into English the names you used for the squishy things I asked about earlier?"

Ariel eyed her over a partially eaten corn cob. "Lion's mane and Portuguese man-of-war."

Karen sucked in her breath. She'd never heard of a lion's mane but she *had* heard of the man-of-war. "Are you telling me that I could have been poisoned out there?"

"Nope. The man-of-war is a rarity around here. Like I said earlier, it would take a pretty big storm to carry it this far north and then for the Gulf Stream to bring it in to shore."

Karen glared at him. "And what about this lion's mane thing?"

Ariel bit into his corn and chewed in exasperating slowness. Karen had an urge to swat him with her mostly demolished lobster tail. Finally, he swallowed and cleared his throat. "Let's see now. Lion's mane. Largest jellyfish in the world, some specimens having been found to be as large as eight feet wide. Contact with tentacles producing severe burns and blisters. Considered highly toxic."

"Ariel!" Now she was definitely angry. "How dare you put me in that kind of danger!"

"There weren't any out there."

"And how, Dr. Singer, do you know that?"

"Because I didn't see any."

Karen fumed over this for a while and then had to admit to herself that she was all in one piece. Besides, she didn't want to be mad at this man. She changed the subject by asking him about his father, hurrying to explain that Susan had told her much of the story short of whether or not father and son had ever been reunited.

Ariel's eyes seemed glazed as, much to her amazement, he told the whole story from his own viewpoint, that of the child and that of the man. Tears glistened in her eyes as he finished by telling her that he and his father had become close friends before his father had died. And then he asked her about her own family.

Karen described life with two doctors for parents and the manner in which she'd always been pushed to achieve higher, more difficult goals. And when she talked of medical school, Greg was a natural addition to the story.

"Tell me about him," Ariel asked. And she did. The way Ariel's smiling eyes looked directly at her was evidence that her life and thoughts truly interested him, and it made it easy to talk about her marriage. The only things she left out were the facts of the marriage bed.

But he seemed to know without her telling him. "He couldn't satisfy you, could he?"

Karen looked over to the smoldering coals in the fireplace and said quietly, "No. I thought it was all my fault."

Ariel reached out and took her hand. "It takes two. But there are also lots of men who don't understand a woman's sexual nature."

Karen couldn't help it. She *had* to know. "Ariel, what is it . . . that *you* understand?"

She thought at first that he wasn't going to answer her question. But then, slowly, he told her about Nicole, the Frenchwoman to whom Jordan had introduced him when he was eighteen. The relationship he'd had with her, he said, was not quite what others believed. They were friends, and in a way, Nicole had taken him under her wing. Because of what had happened to his parents, he'd gone to see Nicole again and again. She understood women so well and he thought she might help him find the answers. Along the way, she'd taught him other things as well.

"Did Nicole play roles with you?" He nodded. "And give you the stone heart?"

"Yes."

"And what did she teach you?"

Ariel probed Karen's eyes with his own as if trying to assure himself that she'd accept what he was about to tell her. "She taught me that much of a woman's sexuality lies in her mind."

"Is that all?"

He leaned very close to her and his breath warmed her lips as he said, "As time goes on, you'll discover *all* that I know." Then his soft, full mouth was nuzzling her own, touching, moving away for brief seconds, and then touching once more.

Karen's breath became uneven as he teased her with his mouth. Ariel used his tongue to barely flick out for a taste of the velvety inside of her lips. She opened her mouth for him, but he drew away and she raised wide and startled eyes to him.

Ariel clasped her hand, pulled her to her feet, and smiled at her with eyes that shone bright even in the growing dusk. "It's time for a story, a love story."

As she climbed the hill, a small fear opened like a thistle in the pit of her stomach. It had been safe out there in the open where observation from a stranger strolling on the beach was always a possibility. When Ariel held the door open for her and she stepped into the blue and green living room, the fear opened out wider, pricking at her lungs and throat.

Ariel closed the door behind him and his form was fuzzy in the twilight of the room. She stood straight and still as he walked toward her, growing larger with increasing proximity. Her heart pounded, but not with excitement. There was a tiny fear and a larger anger, but she didn't know why.

Karen remained stiff, her hands at her sides, as Ariel slid his arms around her, effectively locking her own arms in place. And then Ariel was kissing her and she felt his tongue slipping between her teeth, sliding in farther, deeper, arousing her when she didn't want to be aroused. Why was she here? Why was she letting him do this? When she squirmed and threw her head back away from his kiss, he instantly released her.

Her words came up in a burst of anger. "You . . . you can't play with me, Ariel. I won't let you use me for your games!"

Ariel stood staring at her, seeming to consider her outburst with infinite care. "Yes, I want to play with you, but it's not a game. And I *don't* use women."

Moments passed like years as Karen remained in the same spot staring back at Ariel. Was he lying? Was he trying, as she knew so many men did, to talk her into his bed? Or were his mouth and his gentle eyes telling the truth? And if he *was* telling the truth, then shouldn't she be honest in return? What was *her* truth?

She felt her hands curl up into fists and she listened in surprise to her own words. "Yes, it is a game. It's a game of dominance. Greg played it. It was the only way he could control my intellect, but he rejected me after he got tired of playing."

Ariel's eyebrows formed a painful question as he spoke barely above a whisper. "Is that what you think I'm doing? Playing a game of control and that, once I've won, I'll reject you?"

Karen used the silence as her answer.

His lips smiled, but for the first time since she'd known him, his eyes didn't. "I've already won. I won the savage-Indian game. I controlled you—completely—from the beginning to the end of that one. But I haven't rejected you."

This time Karen used the silence as a time for groping. Yes, he *had* controlled her. But what did he want now? For that matter, what did she herself want?

Suddenly, Ariel turned away from her, walked over to the bookshelves, and switched on the small wall lamp nearby. He moved in front of the shelves, and though his back was turned, Karen knew he was scanning the titles. Abruptly, he reached up, slid a large book off the shelf, and turned back toward her. Before he flipped open the cover, she caught the title: *Explorers, Their Works and Words.*

Ariel ran his eyes down the table of contents. Then, seeming to have found what he wanted, he opened to a particular page, inserted his finger to hold the place, and then grabbed Karen's hand to tug her down to the carpeted floor with him.

He grinned at her resistance. "I'm not going to attack you. Anyway, not with a book. Come on. Sit next to me."

He looked and sounded harmless, for the moment at least. "What's so important in a book about explorers?"

"Sit next to me and I'll tell you."

Once she was settled near Ariel, who had folded his long legs Indian-style as a base for the book, he asked, "Are you familiar with the stories about the Amazon women?"

A pinpoint of fear pricked at her. "Of course. I even know that the legend originated in ancient Greece and not in South America."

"Good." Ariel turned a few pages on which Karen glimpsed pictures of Greek statues. "Then we can dispense with a lot of the preliminaries."

"What preliminaries?"

"Such as the explanation that the Amazons formed a nation in which everything was the wrong way around."

The pinprick of fear was forgotten. "That's one I never heard about."

"Me neither until I read this book. In order to introduce a section here on a Spanish explorer claiming to have fought with Amazons in South America, there's a whole explanation of the early Greek stories."

Not only was the fear forgotten but so was the original reason for which Ariel had brought her up to his cottage. Karen listened intently as he spun out tales of a mythical nation in which turnabout wasn't just fair play—it was a way of life. In this land, it was the men who performed domestic duties and submitted while it was the women who hunted, made war, and aggressively dominated.

As Ariel talked, Karen willingly let him weave the legend around her with his questions of "Can you imagine being the one who wears the quiver and draws the bowstring?" or "What do you suppose it was like to be an Amazonian queen who chose a mate only to subjugate him, use him for his seed, and then toss him away afterward when his services were no longer required?"

The stories Ariel told and the responses his questions elicited in her blended easily with Karen's long-held resentments. She saw herself as that Amazon queen, the epitome of how she'd often felt when, again and again, she had proved to be a strong intellect, stronger than most men she knew. But what about this man? He always seemed at least on a par with her and, sometimes, above.

She didn't notice how Ariel's leg now pressed against hers, not consciously anyway, nor did she notice when exactly he had slipped his arm around her shoulders. However, she *did* notice when he said, "You'd be an irresistible queen of the Amazons. I can imagine myself willingly taking off my clothes"—he unzipped his cutoffs, rose to step out of them, and then lay down prone and naked on the carpet—"and lying at your feet, ready to do your bidding and to have you do to me whatever you desire."

The fantasy of being an Amazon and the sight of this long, golden male body spread out before her accelerated Karen's already quick-tempoed heart. When had it begun beating so rapidly? And how had they arrived at this point in which Ariel lay naked and she quivered with desire?

She didn't care. It was a game—just a game—and she could play, dammit. She had a *right* to play if she wanted to.

And for the first time in her life, Karen allowed her imagination and her sense of play their freedom. She rose to her knees, seeing not a simple cottage room, but a jungle through which she'd been walking to the rhythm of exotic birdsong. She was an Amazon queen with dark, glistening flesh who now shed her garment of leopard skin as she prepared to use this white man who had mistakenly brazened his way into her realm.

But she couldn't hold on to the fantasy. She was too smart for that. Her mind harked back to the telephone conversation they'd had. "Want to to switch?" he'd asked. "I'll let you be the man if you want."

The prickly thistle of fear that had opened inside her began to close, its petals wilting until it was gone. In its place grew a joy like daisies in the sun. Perhaps for her mother she'd had to be like a man, perhaps in med school she'd had to minimize her female side, perhaps for Greg she'd had to let the woman within her lie dormant—but not with Ariel.

Karen looked down at herself. When had she removed her clothes? Then she slid her eyes to Ariel, long and naked at her feet. He lay there, so vulnerable, so . . . giving.

"Ariel, I don't need this game."

His eyes questioned her as he got back to his feet without a word.

She watched his gaze travel her face as if searching for something. Then he lifted his hand to touch the space between her breasts where her heart thump-

thumped in joy and expectation. He left his hand there, looking at it, no doubt feeling her heartsong.

Karen waited until he lifted his eyes to hers. "I don't want to be a little girl captured and I don't want to switch roles so that I'm like a man. I just want to be me, Karen, and I just want you to be Ariel."

Ariel's eyes darkened as if her words had been the drug she used in her office. "Good."

Good? Was that all the man with the golden tongue could say? Well, yes, it *was* good. She smiled. "Now what?"

"Now," he said while turning her toward his bedroom, "Karen and Ariel make love like two ordinary people on an ordinary bed."

His teeth closed soft, then hard, then soft again on the nape of her neck. She almost laughed. His bite was telegraphic, sending shivery messages where she hadn't expected them.

"Ordinary people," he said as they entered the room. "Ordinary bed," he said as they lay down together, hot skin on hot skin. "Extraordinary." The word rode out of him on a sigh.

Unlike their first time on this bed, Ariel was silent. This time, it was Karen who spoke, less aware of her words than of the playful freedom she was feeling for the first time in her life. She wanted to give, give in every possible way to this man with ocean-blue eyes and sunshine-kissed hair. And in return for her gift, she wanted to be allowed to sip at him slowly, to make him last.

Thus, she spoke to him as she bent over him to taste his long calf, telling him he held the flavor of the salty restless sea; she spoke to him as she ran just the tip of her tongue along the inside of his thigh and up onto his taut stomach, telling him that the sound of his moan was like the ocean wind that urged her out, farther and farther.

She felt her feminine strength, her able seduction, and the image of the Amazon grew, flourished, and overtook the visions she'd had of the sea. She became silent. She played with the image of strength, pretending that her hands were shackles wrapped around Ariel's quick-pulsing wrists, that the tongue she darted between his full lips was a secret potion.

But his tongue answered hers and she was losing, and he was rolling her over to pin her down with his body and she was lost, the fantasy gone.

Just Karen and Ariel: Karen lifting her body so he could slip his hand down low and pull her against him to create a burning need deep within.

Just Ariel and Karen: Ariel waiting for her impatient fingers to guide him into the place where the imagined and the real combined into the ongoing, thrusting rhythm of life.

They joined, fractions of an inch at a time, until neither of them could wait any longer. There was a table laid out before them, filled with a feast of salted wet skin and sweet liquid, and they rushed toward it, hungry for every flavor of love.

Karen was full, beyond full. She grew, she swelled until she thought she'd burst. And then she did burst, she spilled as Ariel spilled, and she felt satiated in her body, in her mind. It was then that she spoke her heart.

"I love you. Ariel, I love you."

Silence.

Then his answer that wasn't an answer: "God, Karen, that was beautiful."

A tendril of shame uncurled in her mind but she fought it. She took his hand from the pillow beside her head and opened out his fingers to kiss his moist palm.

The odor of his skin filled her senses and she folded down his fingers as he watched her and she touched his knuckles to her lips.

They were rough. She pushed his hand just far enough away to look at the skin. It looked as if his knuckles had been scraped raw and had only recently begun to heal. It was just as if . . . as if he'd been in a fight. But how could that be? Ariel was many things, but he was certainly not the muscle-head sort.

She glanced up at him. "What happened to your hand?"

It's simple, Karen, Ariel thought as he stared at her lush brown eyes. This highly intelligent man beat the living hell out of someone. Now how was he supposed to tell her that? He'd managed to get her to drop some of her smart-lady armor, but if he told her why his knuckles looked as if he'd been in a barroom brawl, she'd hate him. Hotheaded brutes weren't exactly her type.

"Remember the clam that bit my face?" He watched her eyes flick up to the cut on his cheekbone. "Well, I bit it back." And there you have it, folks, the ultimately stupid answer of the century.

"Come on, Ariel. We've shared an awful lot of ourselves with each other over the past few weeks. You don't have to hide behind jokes."

Her insight stunned him. He'd hidden behind a wall of humor for years, the same way she'd hidden behind her intellect. But if he poured it all out to her, all the anger and all the feelings of being unwanted, unwantable, what would she think of him? One of two things. She'd either be disgusted or . . . or all those damned maternal instincts would come out and she'd feel sorry for him.

A powerfully obscene word reverberated through his

mind. There was a third possibility: she might fall in love with him.

His internal monologue went on hold. He was hearing what she'd said immediately following their sensational lovemaking: "I love you. Ariel, I love you."

This was no good, no good at all. He had to think. He had to find a way to be alone so he could think.

He rolled off her and experienced a moment of profound loss. "I hate to say this, but the combination of lobster for dinner and you for dessert has done nothing spectacular for my digestion." His stomach snarled as if on cue, and he grinned. Karen had no way of knowing his stomach sometimes did that after sex.

Karen couldn't smile in return. She knew beyond all doubt that, as she'd originally suspected, she wasn't able to satisfy a man.

They said little to each other on the way back to Falmouth. At her door, Ariel kissed her lightly on the forehead—why not softly on the lips?—and Karen turned her face away so he wouldn't see the tears glazing her eyes.

He stood there, his arms hanging loosely at his sides. "I'll call you."

Then he was gone and Karen was going into her house, her terribly empty house, and she was lying facedown on her lovely new couch, and she was sobbing into the smooth velvet cushions. She'd made a mistake, she'd made a terrible mistake.

Chapter Seven

Friday. It had always been her favorite day of the week. What had happened to Fridays? Karen sat alone in her kitchen with a half-cup of lukewarm coffee suspended before her in her hands. She looked at it. Had she been about to drink or had she done so already? She couldn't remember and she didn't want it anymore anyway; Friday morning had ruined its flavor. It tasted as bitter as her thoughts had been throughout the sleepless night.

She'd gone over and over the events of the day before in her mind, trying desperately to sort them out, to place them in a logical order that might solve the question of why Ariel had suddenly drawn away from her. At first, she'd decided that he'd merely been using her for the satisfaction of his own lust. But this answer simply made no sense. His nature was too gentle, too caring. It had to be something else. After all, he'd come to the office the day before asking *her* out, he'd come in search of her. She hadn't thrown herself at him, not once. Or had she?

In the small hours of the morning, she'd heard her own voice ringing in her head: "I love you. Ariel, I love you." That was the mistake she'd made.

Yes, she had thrown herself at him. She'd thrown her entire soul at him. Karen set her coffeecup down and buried her face in her hands. Was it wrong to love him?

An image of Ariel drifted into her mind, a vivid memory of him standing on the beach, his body drying in the ocean wind. She had been standing between Ariel and the water and was looking up at him. She still remembered having to squint because the setting sun had been behind him.

Now, as she sat in her immaculate red-and-white kitchen, she saw Ariel once again with the air flowing through his hair, lifting strands of it to be touched by the sunlight, illuminated by it. His golden hair had shimmered like a halo and she remembered how she'd once again been reminded of an angel, a beautiful angel man. At that moment, she'd wanted to walk forward, to have him absorb her body into his so that she could be one with him, so that she could be a part of his exquisite being.

"Oh, my God!" Karen sobbed into the darkness of her palms, thinking to herself how right that was: to her, he was indeed a god.

But it was time to go into the office, to take care of her patients. She stood up, wiped at the hopeless tears on her face, and breathed in deeply. Yes, it was time to once again be the smart lady. It was also time to stop being a woman in the fathomless depths of love.

By the time she'd walked into the waiting room, Fran was unlocking the outer door and coming in. The older woman said good morning with her usual cheerful smile, but the smile dissolved in an instant. "Dr. Watts, you'll have to excuse me for saying so, but you look horrid. Have you been sick?"

Yes. Lovesick. "No, I'm just suffering from a bit of insomnia."

Even though she felt as bad as she no doubt looked, the rest of the day ran with resolute smoothness until Manny Rivera came in at four o'clock.

"Hi." Manny grinned at her, his teeth very white in contrast to his black, wavy hair and deeply tanned skin.

"Hi, Manny. How're things going?" She grinned back at him. She liked Manny, a man-child so close to full adulthood and yet still showing all the innocence of youth.

Manny eased back into the examining chair. "Everything's fine. It's as if nothing ever happened to my eye."

Karen finished examining him, and then, because he was the last patient of the day and because she liked him, she drew him into friendly conversation with a question. "How are your studies going?"

"Great, though I'm not sure any of it would have been so easy without Dr. Singer."

"Why's that?" Did she really want to know?

"Well, for one thing, he spent a lot of time this past week helping me catch up on my work." Manny paused and stared straight at Karen. "For another, he paid my hospital bill for me—I mean, as a loan. Dr. Watts, you said the bill would be no problem."

Karen thought of how she and Ariel had assured Manny that the only problem was getting his eye repaired. She also thought of how she'd never submitted her own bill to Manny so that there'd be only that of the hospital to pay. She looked down at her hands, which rubbed together nervously in her lap. "Is it a problem?"

"Kind of. I don't know when I'll be able to pay back the money to him."

Karen looked back up at Manny with a sudden realization. "Are you sure he *wants* to be paid back?"

"What do you mean?"

Karen was silent for a moment, and then, choosing

her words with care, she said, "Did you know that Dr. Singer's work is probably very lucrative?"

Manny cocked his head to the side. "No, but what's that got to do with the fact that I owe him?"

Again, Karen's words were carefully chosen. "Manny, Dr. Singer is a special sort of person. He . . . he likes to help people and I'm not sure he wants anything in return for it when he's done." That was it. She hadn't realized it until she'd completed her own sentence. Ariel had simply been helping her. First, he'd pulled her out of her intellectual shell through the savage-Indian fantasy, then he'd somehow understood all her anger and hostilities and had set about helping her work it all out through the Amazon scene.

Karen came out of her startling reverie to hear Manny saying, "It doesn't make any difference. I still owe him. He spent his money on me and he spent Monday through Wednesday helping me study." Manny looked past Karen. "Boy! Am I ever going to miss him."

Karen's heart skipped a beat. "What do you mean?"

"He took off for the Bahamas. He got on the plane a few hours ago."

Her heart skipped a second beat and her stomach drew in on itself. All she could say was one word. "Why?"

"I guess he decided at the last minute that he needed some vacation time. Seems he's going to meet a friend down there who's also an oceanographer."

"What are they going to do?"

Manny's whole demeanor was one of painful yearning. "Exactly what I'd like to do—go to San Salvador and scuba-dive."

Karen was pleased with only one thing: she was managing to keep her voice devoid of the trembling she felt inside. "I wonder why he decided, as you say, to go at the last minute."

Manny shook his head. "I don't know. I guess he really needed a vacation. Though it's kind of like—what do you call it?—a busman's holiday."

"How's that?"

Manny smiled. "He's going to be studying the area where the coast drops off down into the deep blue sea. It's the same as if you took a vacation by going into a research lab for ophthalmology and stayed there for a month."

Karen didn't want to ask but she had to know. "Is that how long he'll be down there?"

Manny laughed. "Well, I don't think he'll be in the water for a month, but yeah, that's about how long he thought he'd be gone. Now that I think of it, he mentioned something about looking into a job offer at the Miami Institute. If it looked good, he said he might not come back at all." A cloud of emotion glided across Manny's dark eyes. "As much as I wish the best for Dr. Singer, I also hope he comes back. He's been like brother and father all rolled up into one for me."

A half-hour later, Karen closed the office section's door behind her, but she stood for a moment with her hand still on the knob. A month. He'd be gone a month—or forever. Was it her fault? Was Ariel trying to escape her as if she were some ocean monster bent on destroying the beautiful sea god? Or maybe it wasn't that at all. Maybe, just maybe she'd overrated him and his motives. He may have known all along that he'd be joining his friend—Jordan, for sure—down in the Bahamas and that there was a strong possibility of his moving from Cape Cod. And maybe, too, she'd only been an object of his scientific mind's curious nature. What had she read about such minds? They recognized a problem, and as soon as they did, they couldn't keep themselves from analyzing and studying the anomaly until a solution had occurred to them.

Karen loosened her tight grip on the doorknob and pivoted slowly, then walked down the short hall that led to both the kitchen and the living room. Cold rooms, sterile rooms, rooms whose greatest characteristic was their emptiness.

But they weren't entirely empty.

Ariel was standing with his back to her, facing the framed photographs on the mantel above the spotlessly clean fireplace.

She stopped short in the doorway. "H-how did you get in?"

He spun around on his heel, surprise in the angle of his eyebrows but something quite different, something undefinable in his eyes. It reminded Karen of fear. He smiled and the look was gone.

"Do you always leave your front door unlocked?"

Had she forgotten to lock the door last night? Probably. She'd cried herself into fitful sleep on the couch.

What was she supposed to say to him? What did he want? "Manny told me a little while ago that you were leaving. He made it sound as if you were already gone."

"I almost was." Ariel glanced back at the framed photographs. "Is this your family?"

"Yes." She didn't want to talk about her family. She wanted to talk about Karen and Ariel. But was there anything to talk about? Everything had happened inside her while he seemed to have been left untouched. "Ariel, I'm sure you didn't sneak into my house to look at photographs."

"I didn't sneak in. I turned the doorknob and *walked* in."

"Okay, so you walked in. Nevertheless, you didn't

come here to look at pictures of my parents and my sister."

Ariel's expression was as bland as oatmeal. "This is Liza? She's very pretty."

His simple, factual statement shot pain throughout her whole being. "Yes, she's the pretty one." Karen swallowed hard against the pain and forced herself to look directly at Ariel. "You'd probably like Liza." Too late to stop herself, she added, "She's terrified of getting tied down."

Karen remained where she was, utterly bewildered when Ariel strode quickly over to her and wrapped his long, strong arms around her. It felt like love, but she knew it wasn't, and so she left her arms as they were, rigid at her sides. Even so, she could sense his heart banging with life inside him and she luxuriated in the feel of it and in the vibrant heat spreading into her from his body. If only he loved her. If only she could put her arms around him and tell him how his warm skin was cause enough for addiction, how his almond eyes could stop the breath in her, and how—most important of all—how the twists and turns of his mind could fill an entire lifetime with joy and wonder.

"Maybe I would," he said softly in her ear. "Maybe I'd like Liza, but if I did, it wouldn't be because she was pretty or because ... Dammit!" He dropped his arms away from her, stepped back, and fixed his gaze on her. A small pulse ticked at his temple. "I'd like her, Karen, because she's *your* sister."

"Stupid reason."

A second passed in which Karen and Ariel both hung there, suspended in a space where time was meaningless. He'd spoken truth; she'd rejected it for lack of belief in herself.

Ariel waited. He was sure his brain would start

working again any minute now. Stupid reason? Was it so stupid to like everything about Karen? Well, maybe it *was* stupid. Maybe *he* was stupid. He felt pretty stupid.

He wanted to laugh, to blow away this entire episode in his life with a great purge of laughter and then go back to the very beginning when he'd stood writing a check in Karen's office. He could have kept this tangle of emotions from happening if he hadn't followed her into this part of the house. And even if he *had* gone this far, he still could have stopped because, on that first day, he hadn't loved her yet.

No, that was wrong. He didn't love Karen. One person couldn't fall in love with another in less than three weeks. It took longer. Was there a rule for love, some kind of equation? he wondered. Take the mass of two falling bodies, multiply by number of days gone by, divide by x number of faults . . .

Ariel grinned. "What do you consider your worst fault?"

Karen's eyes were dark and moist. "You."

He swallowed the grin. Her answer was one of those unexpected factors that scientists are supposed to expect. He'd been a complete scientific dimwit in the past few weeks. It had to stop. He was an MIT cum-laude graduate. A graduate, too, of Woods Hole Oceanographic Institution. Most people only got to go there on tour. And he'd already developed the first part of a sensational career, one in which he might be on the Cape for a month, in California the next, and in Australia the one after that. A traveler just like his father. He didn't want to repeat Joshua Singer's mistake.

"You're right, Karen. I'm a great big fault in your

life." And you're just as big a fault in mine. "That's why I'm here instead of on a plane to the Bahamas."

God, Karen, do you know what it does to me when you stand there so tall and full of dignity and curves and promises of sweet-smelling skin? Do you know?

Karen's mouth seemed smaller and her eyes larger. "Ariel, why *are* you here? What do you want from me?"

I want to feel your body all warm beneath mine. "I don't know."

"You must have had some reason for coming here."

Ariel felt the uncontrollable rise of desire. She was so heartbreakingly beautiful. Sure, her features were perhaps a bit too angular for some men's tastes, but they suited him just fine. Aristocratic, almost haughty. Like visions of an English schoolmistress. Ah, but it was the contrast of her looks with all that softness inside that really dazzled him.

"I came because . . ." His heart was pounding up into his throat and he knew that if he didn't walk out this minute he was going to employ every method known to man to seduce this woman.

He mustn't do this, he thought. But his arm was moving and he watched in fascination as it raised up, reached out toward Karen, touched a tear trailing down her cheek, brought the tiny drop that glistened on his fingertip to his lips. The tear was perfectly seasoned with the salt of life.

No, you can't do this. But he was doing it anyway, he was reaching out again, pulling her to him, pressing her hard against his demanding body. He couldn't stop himself. Ariel could feel the losing battle mirrored in her body, the way it was so pliant against his.

As he dropped his head, he intended the kiss to be tender, but her lips were hot and supple on his and it unleashed him. He wanted to plunge all of himself into all of her, and it made the kiss hurt. He heard her moan and he knew she felt the pain as he did—a wild, undeniable need.

His hands shook as he found the zipper on the back of her dress and opened it. The hooks of her bra came apart between his searching fingers and then, still in the depths of her sweet mouth, he pulled, almost ripped, the dress down from her shoulders so he could place his hands on her soft, full breasts.

Ariel felt the beads of sweat gluing his hair to his temples and he felt his pulse racing as if toward the end of the world. He had to hold on. He couldn't just take her right here on the floor like some kind of animal. But what was she doing to him, pulling away like that, unbuttoning his shirt with rapid fingers, scraping her teeth down his chest to his belly? Oh so good, it felt so . . . good.

Control was gone. He flung away his clothes while Karen did the same. There was no time, no thought of seeking the comfort of couch or bed. He sank with her onto the plush carpet.

Now it was real. Her body was beneath his and, yes, it was moist and willing like he knew it would be.

Hold on, Ariel. Don't just take. But it was no good. Her body reflected every bit of his own urgency. Her rhythm was driving him beyond all recall, and he was the raging beast in the jungle demanding relief.

He felt himself surging out and into her, and for a single moment he wasn't aware of Karen—just this victorious, surging ecstasy.

His breathing slowed, then thought trickled back in. Had he satisfied her? Should he ask?

Awareness spread further. What had happened? He'd come here to say good-bye. This wasn't how you said good-bye. This was how you hurt another person. He was hurting Karen, only she didn't know it yet.

Carefully, Ariel lifted himself up. He didn't want to look at her, but he couldn't help it. In her eyes was all the love and yearning he knew he'd see. He looked away.

He floundered about in his mind for an easy way out of all this. He found nothing, so he sat up, pulling Karen up with him. He'd have to tell the truth. Or at least some small part of it.

"Karen, I didn't mean for this to happen."

The skin tightened beneath her brown eyes. "Neither did I. I thought you came here to say good-bye."

"I did."

"Is this how you usually do it?"

Every bit of her pain showed. What on earth had he done? "No. I meant to . . . to tell you I was going down to San Salvador for a while. That's in the Bahamas, you know, and . . ." You idiot! You're starting to ramble! "And anyway, after that I'm going to look into a possible job in Miami."

She stood up, moved away from him, and he felt suddenly very remote and isolated, as if the last friend he had in the world had just died.

Ariel got to his feet and mutely watched her gather up her clothes before walking away toward the stairs. She stopped, one foot already on the bottom step, her hand gripping the banister. Her eyes were empty, completely empty.

Ariel felt as if he'd just committed a crime. Guilt surged through him such as he'd never felt before. And her final words were dry, just like his soul.

"You let yourself in. I think you can let yourself out, too."

Opposing thoughts and emotions hung in Karen's

mind like magnets repelling one another. She remained at the top of the stairs, her clothes falling unnoticed to the floor, as she listened to the distant, empty sounds of Ariel dressing. She heard the faint swish of pants drawn up over long legs, then the sharper snap and zip as he closed them. She thought of those legs, how she'd never see them again, but she refused entrance to the emotion accompanying this knowledge. Instead, she concentrated on the pants. They'd been a lightweight gabardine, chocolate-colored cotton, stylishly pleated at the waistband. Was the shirt he'd worn tucked into that waistband a rich yellow? Was it the same as his hair, was it the shade of summer sunshine?

Footsteps approached softly on the carpet below. What kind of shoes had he been wearing? She heard him calling, dove-quiet, "Karen?" But she didn't answer. And then he called again just as before and, again, she didn't answer.

The opening of the door chased a draft up the stairs. Karen shivered. Then the draft was gone as the door clicked shut. She whispered, "I love you," to the surrounding walls and floors, but no one heard her, not even herself, because she was afraid to listen. The loss was too great.

Without bothering to dress, she went downstairs to the kitchen, picked up the telephone receiver, dialed a number she knew by heart, and waited for the familiar voice to answer.

"Hi, Susan. You're going to have company for the weekend."

Chapter Eight

❦

Karen watched raindrops weeping down the multi-paned, second-story windows of Susan's Beacon Street apartment. Then she remembered how it had rained that first night when she and Ariel had sat in his car and he'd said he was as relentless as a molecule of water in the ocean. In the following days, he'd single-mindedly searched for the warmth within her, found it, then left her painfully exposed. She wished she could say she hated him, but the words wouldn't come. Karen slid her gaze from the nighttime windows over to Susan.

"Aha!" Susan pulled a sagging shoe box from the cabinet beneath an age-scarred bookcase and looked over her shoulder to the floral couch where Karen sat burrowing her finger into a hole where a button had once been.

"I found just what two women on a dateless Friday night need." Susan sank down next to Karen on the dilapidated couch. "You have a choice. It's either this box or go out on the town and get spectacularly drunk. And sick."

"Before I choose," Karen said, "tell me what's in the box."

"Memories."

Karen's mind was already a stagnant bog of memories. On top of that, Susan's penchant for other people's memories in the form of Salvation Army furniture wasn't as amusing as usual. Tonight the comfortably worn furniture gave off an aura that was much too homey, an atmosphere in which it was easy to conjure up a young wife waiting on the couch, green crayon scribbled on the wall, and a man walking through the door and calling, "Hi, honey. I'm home."

Karen forcefully switched off the pictures in her mind. The husband had looked too much like Ariel. "What do you mean, a box full of memories?"

"Pictures. This box is my version of a photo album." Susan removed the lid, and a few of the top photographs skidded out onto the worn Oriental carpet.

Karen hoped she appeared genuinely casual each time during the next hour when a snapshot of Ariel was plucked from the box. Out of order, she saw a scrawny, pubescent boy who smiled; a seven-year-old whose teeth seemed too large who smiled; a boy in his late teens who was already heartbreakingly handsome who smiled. Ariel smiling. Ariel grinning. Ariel laughing.

The photograph she now held was of Susan's mother. On one side of Mrs. Mathews was a hip-high Ariel grinning over at the other side of his aunt, where a chubby little Susan stood scowling and picking her nose. It was a typical picture of how children behave before the camera, a funny picture, but Karen wasn't amused. She was thinking of how fear disguised itself.

"Susan, have you ever seen Ariel cry? I mean, in the years after his mother died?"

"I don't know." Susan paused for less than a second. "No. I don't think he even cried at his mother's funeral. . . . Odd. Even ten-year-old boys cry. I've watched them do it in my office."

Karen continued thinking of Ariel's lack of tears

while Susan went back to describing the circumstances surrounding the various photographs.

"Gee." Susan stared at the very last picture. "I didn't know this was in here," she said slowly.

Karen saw Ariel, standing on a beach with a tall, black-haired beauty. "Who's she?" He couldn't have been more than eighteen, yet she was jealous.

"Nicole. Nicole Bouchard."

Karen tucked the name away in her mind. She was going to need it.

Ariel zipped up the wet suit's vest. It felt warm, too warm, as he stood on the deck of the boat bathed in the glare of late-afternoon sunlight. But he knew it would feel good to have the vest on at a hundred feet down. Better at two hundred feet. He looked over at Jordan, who stood nearby, and saw that his friend was already attaching his weight belt, adjusting it over a hard, muscle-broadened body. Jordan. It was so damned good to be with him again.

Only a week had gone by since he'd last seen him, but Jordan could be the best medicine in the world. Maybe this Arab devil could help him cure a critical case of *Homo ignoramus.*

Ariel stood quietly, gratefully allowing Sam, who wasn't diving today, to help him into the scuba. Then he attached the weight belt himself. He looked up from his belt to see Jordan shifting from one foot to the other, watching with a grin on his square, mustached face. Ariel smiled back at him. He knew what the grin meant. Jordan should never have bothered with an education. He'd been smart enough for it, though Ariel had outshone him during those years spent in the classroom. It wasn't that. Jordan had always spent every available minute underwater. It was a wonder he hadn't sprouted fins and gills. The smile smeared across Jordan's face was merely the anticipation welling up in him once again. It was really a dolphin's grin.

Simultaneously, Ariel and Jordan put their mouthpieces in place, closed their teeth on the nibs, and breathed a few times to check the air. Jordan gave Ariel the OK sign of a circle with his thumb and forefinger. Ariel returned it.

The air was OK, but was everything else? No, now wasn't the time to consider other things. It was not the time to weigh the pros and cons of taking the job at the Miami Institute. He was about to dive into some of the most beautiful waters and that should be all that was on his mind.

Jordan made an attempt to bow and sweep his arm in a gesture indicating that Ariel should be his guest and enter the water first, but the tanks were too heavy and Ariel caught his friend just before Jordan made what would have been an unusual entry into San Salvador's waters. Ariel controlled his desire to laugh. The flange of his mouthpiece between his lips and teeth discouraged a sense of humor.

The boat was set up for diving, and Ariel, at Jordan's almost disastrous request, squatted on the low platform first, putting his hands on his mask to keep it in place. He leaned back, allowing the weight of his tanks to pull him down into a back-roll entry. He watched his flippered feet flying up over his head as he tumbled, and then he was underwater. He inhaled and breathed out of his nose to force the water that had seeped into his mask out through the purge valve.

He waited until Jordan was next to him before bending his knees and tilting down. Extending his legs,

Ariel felt the water stroke his face as he headed down to the coral reefs. But, unlike this morning, they would go farther down, beyond the edge where the reef met the deep, open sea.

Ariel was torn between the desire to repeat that morning's exploration of the beautiful, variegated marine life of the coral reef and to go deeper. He stopped to stare into the face of a Nassau grouper—a two-footer, Ariel estimated. The fish approached looking grumpy and hungry. Sorry, Ariel thought, I only let pretty eye doctors taste my skin. The thought and his immediate response to it sent him away from the grouper. Other things. He had to think of other things. Where was all his intelligence? Where was the brainpower that had once sent him single-mindedly to the top of his class in everything?

He angled deeper, stopped again, and looked around for his friend. Jordan was no more than ten feet away, suspended in the water, flippers held horizontal as if he were standing on a hard surface. He had his hands firmly planted on his hips in an attitude of severely tried patience. God! He wished Jordan wouldn't do things like that underwater. Ariel held his breath and pictured his father so he could avoid laughing. It didn't pay to laugh around a mouthpiece. He'd done it once— Jordan's fault—and he'd lost the mouthpiece and had drunk salt water. How long ago had that been? Nine, ten years ago? No matter. He was still a young man. Thirty-one. Too young to decide between commitment to himself and to another. Well, he *was* too young, wasn't he?

Ariel looked up briefly. Light was coming in from all directions. How deep was he? He looked at his depth gauge. Sixteen meters. A little over fifty-two feet.

Before he was out of the water today, he'd have multiplied that measure by four.

Okay, he thought, let's get on with it. Maybe the pressure at two hundred feet will squeeze the Colonial girl-cum-Amazon into a tight little ball that I can toss away.

But at seventy feet, Ariel's mind was still on Karen. Then, he came to the edge of a world and Karen's image was gone. He hung there feeling as if he were on the roof of a skyscraper. Here, the coral was like a cliff dropping off abruptly into the fathomless blue. The very sheerness of the drop made him giddy. He wasn't deep enough yet to be feeling the effects of nitrogen narcosis, rapture of the deep.

From here, he descended quickly, with Jordan doing the same nearby. They stopped at two hundred feet. Ariel grabbed a feathery clump of black coral and glanced up. The reef was a shadowy edge slicing across the surface glimmer. Then he looked down. The blue dissolved into a black abyss where there would be no direction, no up, no down.

He felt good—too good. He recognized the beginnings of nitrogen narcosis. Jacques Cousteau is prone to it, too. I'm in good company, he thought. But wouldn't it be nice to just stay down here, to be stupidly happy with no problems, no decisions to make? No Karen to haunt me?

Ariel spent a few more minutes watching the fish, peering at the algae and coral, and then signaled to Jordan that he was starting up. Making a twirling motion toward his head with his forefinger, he indicated that he was experiencing a most dangerous form of happiness. Rapture of the deep had drowned better men than he.

*   *   *

"I left my spare key on the kitchen table in case you feel like going out for a while." Susan stopped on her way out the door and gave Karen a long, considering look. "Listen. It's obvious that something's bugging you. Why don't you take a walk? Go over to Quincy Market and buy a crazy hat you'd never wear in a million years."

Karen faked a casual yawn. "Maybe I'll just take a deliciously long nap."

"Not such a bad idea either by the look of you. Didn't you sleep last night?"

This time, Karen's yawn was genuine. "Strange bed."

"You're a liar." Susan grinned. "Anyway, I should be back no later than five. Sorry about having to work. Now, if you'd called the day *before* yesterday, I might have been able to—"

"Don't worry about it. I'll be fine. Go on before all your patients disappear."

The door closed on Susan's final words: "Wish they would."

No sooner was Susan out the door than Karen was up and heading into the kitchen for the telephone directory she knew Susan kept on top of the refrigerator.

She'd argued with herself most of the night about doing this. One part of her asked what possible good it could do to talk with Nicole. Another part answered that it could do lots of good. She needed to know at least *why* Ariel had run away just when it felt as if he might be falling in love with her. Karen was sure that, if anyone was going to know the answer, it would be Nicole Bouchard.

She ran her finger down an appallingly long list of Bouchards. It hadn't occurred to her how common a

French name it was. However, tucked in between a Michael and a Paul Bouchard was an N. Bouchard. N for Nicole?

Repeating the phone number aloud, she picked up the receiver, pressed the first digit, heard the electronic tone, then hung up. Going back to the still-open directory, Karen copied down the address on the back of a grocery receipt. Nicole—if that was who N. Bouchard was—didn't live very far from Beacon Street.

Karen spared only a few minutes to pull her hair up neatly on top of her head and to apply a little powder to conceal the dark rings beneath her eyes. She wanted to look good but she didn't want to fuss with herself so long that she had enough time to lose her nerve. She needed answers too desperately to let that happen.

It turned out to be a longer walk than she'd calculated, but the activity helped use up some of the excess adrenaline her system had pumped out in preparation for this possible meeting.

There it was. The same number as she'd written on the grocery receipt. Just to be sure, she took the slip of paper out of her skirt pocket. Yes, this was the address.

She stayed where she was, caught up in the sight of a small group of children playing hopscotch on the sidewalk. Had she played hopscotch when she was little?

A girl of about seven saw Karen watching and she stopped midhop, a cherub's smile lighting her soft features. "Wanna play with us?"

Karen laughed. "Darned if I wouldn't love to. But I can't, sweetheart. I have an appointment to keep."

Then she was climbing concrete steps, walking into the apartment building, and reading the names on the mailboxes situated just inside the door. Apartment 3B. Up the stairs. This one? No, that's 3A. There it is.

Knock. Come on, you've gone too far to chicken out now.

Karen lifted her perspiring hand to the door, rapped twice, waited, and was just turning to leave when the door opened.

"Yes?"

Karen turned back to see a woman whose photographs didn't do her a bit of justice. Even in her late forties, Nicole Bouchard was exquisite.

Ariel knew he was still a hundred feet beneath the surface and that his first decompression stop wouldn't occur until he was up to thirty feet. But it was so beautiful right on the edge of the reef that he stopped. Jordan rose past him and motioned for him to follow. In a minute, friend, he thought.

Suddenly, Jordan's rising figure was blotted out by an enormous school of fish. Ariel was mezmerized by the bodies shimmering all around him. It was fantastic!

He was about to start up again when a huge body flashed past him. Spotted dolphin. Wow! Haven't seen one of them in a long time.

Ariel turned to watch as the dolphin swam through the school of fish, eating as it went. Wasteful slob. He watched pieces of half-eaten fish floating down and away from the dolphin. But then, why pick up the pieces when there's always more straight ahead? Like more women in the future? No, you damned fool, you know better than that. That's not your style.

Another large body skimmed past him, almost touching his arm. Ariel turned quickly and saw that he was not only in the path of a school of fish, but also in the way of a school of spotted dolphins. And they were all eating—and they were all being just as sloppy about it as the first dolphin. Chunks of fish floated around Ariel and he watched as the head of a dead fish drifted down and lodged itself on his air hose. He started to lift his hand to remove the gory item, but he never got the chance to do it.

He caught a movement in front of him and stopped his hand as he looked up and saw what was speeding toward him. *No!*

The tiger shark was snapping up the dolphins' leftovers and one of those leftovers was on Ariel's air hose.

It took only a second. The shark's teeth were only inches from Ariel's face. The jaws closed, the head jerked and pulled, the mouthpiece was yanked from Ariel's mouth, and then . . . the shark was gone.

Time stopped as Ariel held the huge and lucky breath he'd taken when the shark had come in at him. He reached for the hose. It was gone. Shark food.

Think Ariel. Think very carefully. Jordan, where's Jordan? No, no time to look for him. Ariel ripped off his weight belt and kicked powerfully. The bends, he cried inwardly. I'm going to get the goddamned bends!

He hung on to what wits he had left and let the air out of his lungs slowly as he shot up through the bright-aqua water. He wanted desperately to hang on to every bit of air he had in him, but he knew better. He wanted to live. If he surfaced with his lungs full, they would expand further with the decreasing pressure and they'd burst.

It was a lifetime of minutes as he arrowed straight up through the water, past Jordan without even looking at him, up, up, and then he was breaking the surface near the boat. Ariel's first breath of fresh air was an audible wail slicing inward. He pushed the air back out, gasped in again, and as he reached up to Sam's waiting hand, he shouted, "Get me into decompression—fast!"

* * *

"I—I'm Karen Watts. You don't know me, but we have a mutual friend. Ariel Singer."

Nicole's smile revealed a few lines that hadn't been noticeable at first. The lines disappeared along with the smile as she leaned forward on the partially open door and studied Karen long enough to moisten the younger woman's clenched hands with perspiration.

"The look in your eyes," Nicole said with only a trace of French accent, "is that of someone who is much more than his friend."

"Yes. Well, you see—"

"No, no, no." Nicole held up her hand to stop Karen's words. "Come in and join me for a glass of wine." She opened the door wide. "Do you prefer red or white?"

Karen didn't want any wine but she was too polite to refuse. She stepped through the door, smiled as best she could, and said, "White . . . if you have it."

"But of course. Make yourself comfortable while I get it."

Karen stood for a moment, turning slowly to take in the decor of Nicole's living room. It wasn't what she'd expected. Where were the plush red carpet, the floor-to-ceiling brocade draperies, the velvet wallpaper? Where, too, was the cloyingly sweet odor of cheap perfume? White walls, mossy green carpet, gold-and-green furniture, and an atmosphere of bright airiness didn't fit her preconceived notion of a . . .

"Please. Sit down." Nicole glided into the room holding two small wineglasses.

Karen chose the nearest chair and accepted the wine while noticing that Nicole wore a lightweight summer bathrobe. It was the middle of the afternoon. Had she been . . . working all night?

Nicole sat on the end of the couch nearest Karen, took a small sip of her wine, then placed the glass carefully on the coffee table. "Please excuse my state of dress. I've only been out of bed a half-hour."

Karen's eyes widened. Wine for breakfast?

Nicole laughed, a melodic sound. "Mine's apple juice," she said, pointing to her glass. "I cheated."

Karen looked. Sure enough, the color of the liquid in Nicole's glass was too dark to be wine and, suddenly, Karen found herself liking Nicole in spite of the woman's profession.

"Well, Karen Watts, friend of Ariel Singer, how can I help you?"

Nicole's quick smile made her large eyes glow and tinged her high cheekbones with pink. She seemed such an open woman, seemed to offer such an easy friendship, that Karen forgot her wine in favor of telling her story.

It took time in the telling. Karen wanted to make sure Nicole understood all the circumstances, including her repressive upbringing. It was more difficult explaining how Ariel had charmed her into his bed, but Nicole's encouraging words of "Ah, yes" and "But of course" reassured Karen and she told the complete story, even the final chapter, which seemed to have occurred eons ago, though she knew that hardly twenty-four hours had passed since Ariel said goodbye.

"You are deeply in love with him, no?"

"Yes."

"I would say"—Nicole paused as if to lay weight on what came next—"that our poor, sweet Ariel is just as deeply in love with you."

"But—"

"No, don't interrupt me. It is now my turn."

Nicole spoke slowly at first, quickening her pace only after becoming more involved in her memories of Ariel Singer, memories of a boy trying his best to become a man.

Before sealing Ariel into the decompression chamber, Sam said, "I remember the time I was in this damned tank. It was quite an experience being completely alone with just Sam for company . . . I'll check on you in a while. Try to sleep."

Ariel looked up at Sam, who was silhouetted against the backdrop of a quickly darkening sky, and narrowed his eyes. The pain was already beginning. Nitrogen bubbles were forming in his body. "Sam, close it. I hurt."

Then he was alone. Ariel could hear the hiss of air being pumped into the cramped chamber and he concentrated on the sound and breathed deeply, trying to relax against the knives of pain in his legs and lower back. Would he be recompressed in time? Or would he limp through the rest of his tomorrows?

Darkness pressed in on him along with the air. Gradually, the pain lifted—the bubbles were being squeezed back into solution. As the last hint of pain disintegrated, Ariel became aware of how very much alone he really was.

Just Ariel, just me and Ariel Singer. He closed his eyes and found there was no difference. The only way he could tell that his eyes were closed was by the sensation of upper and lower lids meeting. He opened his eyes again and saw the shark bearing down on him, the teeth were long, sharp—and deadly.

His lips formed silent obscenities. God! That sucker

was inches away from my neck. Why aren't I dead? I ought to be dead.

Ariel tried to think about other things, about the grouper he'd seen, about Jordan and their years together in college, about anything except what he'd just been through. Yet it returned. In this powerful darkness that now surrounded him, the vision of the shark coming at him was hallucinatory.

If I can't run from it, he thought, I might as well face it. All right, Dr. Singer, what actually happened? You got in the way. That's all. With some narcosis still remaining, you hung there like a damned fool in a trance watching a gang of fish. No way of knowing that dolphins followed. Sharks like to trail after feeding dolphins—that's something I already knew. But did I have the time to even consider the possibility? Maybe. There's no way of telling how far behind the dolphins the shark was. Stupid. That's all. I was stupid. . . .

His inner voice was silent for only a moment before beginning again. And scared. Admit it, Ariel, you were terrified. A coward? No time to be a coward. Besides, if I'd had the time to be a coward, my air hose wouldn't have been torn apart. No, cowardice belongs in the realm of self-preservation. I had no more time to be a coward than I did to be brave.

Ariel let his mind go blank. For a few seconds, there were no internal conversations, no visions. Just Ariel. Then, out of the dark in his mind, a new vision floated toward him.

With you I had the time. Oh, hell, Karen, you don't know how sorry I am. I was terrified of dying down there in the water. That's the first time I've faced death. Now I can see that, with you, I was a true coward. Ridiculous. I ran from you, but I just waited while a shark nearly did me in.

Yeah. Now there's a definite case of cowardice. And because of my own chickenhearted idiocy, I may have lost the biggest treasure of all. I didn't mean to hurt you, Karen. Did you know that? Ariel's eyes filled with tears. There was no one there to see and he let them come. Deep inside, he hurt too much to keep up any façade of so-called manliness. Sometime later, he slept.

The noise of the chamber being opened woke him. He saw Jordan smiling down at him.

"How are you, buddy?"

Ariel smiled back at him. "Alive."

"Sam said you were attacked by a shark. Christ! I've never personally known anyone who was attacked. Circled maybe, but . . ." Jordan stopped talking while he helped Ariel out of the narrow chamber.

"I wasn't really attacked," Ariel said. He stretched. He felt good. "I just got in the way. If you stepped into traffic and a tractor trailer ran you down, you couldn't really say the truck willfully attacked you, could you?"

"Maybe not," Sam interrupted from a few feet away, "but I'd sure as hell hate that truck."

Jordan laughed. "Let's get off this boat. I've gotta get you into a hospital to be checked over. Ready to have a vicious technician come at you with bloodlust in his eyes?"

"I'm okay. I'm just cold. Where'd you hide my clothes?" Ariel felt pressed. There was something he had to do, and now it wasn't he who was in the way of anything else; something was in *his* way. "I don't need the hospital."

Jordan swore, using one very clear, very loud obscenity. "If Sam and I have to tie you in knots, stuff you in a duffel bag, and drag you there, that's what we'll do. You're going to the hospital."

An hour later, a pretty lab technician tore open the

sterile package containing a syringe. "I hope you don't mind needles. A lot of men—"

"I don't mind," Ariel interrupted. "I know. More men faint than women. Why do you suppose that is?"

The woman's hand poised midway to Ariel's arm as she looked into his eyes. "Maybe it's genetic."

Ariel eyed the long, slender, terribly sharp needle. "Maybe not." Was he scared of a needle? He couldn't help himself and he watched in morbid fascination as the needle slipped under his skin. As he noted the blood slowly filling the syringe, he thought of how it might feel to be a fully expanded balloon with a pin coming at him.

Men don't faint—they deflate, he thought. They hold in so many of their emotions that they become inflated with them like a balloon. All it takes is one tiny pinprick. He remembered Karen's face the last time he'd seen her and then he remembered the shark's teeth. Well, something a bit larger than a pinprick.

It had been a long night. The three men let the large glass door of the hospital swing shut behind them. The sun blazed down at them and they all squinted and turned away from it.

Sam rubbed his eyes. "It's past time for this member of the Three Stooges to hit the hay. What about you guys?"

Jordan threw a friendly arm around Ariel. "As soon as I've heard the rest of this fellow's fish story."

Ariel and Jordan stood there for a moment watching Sam walk down the cement steps, their thoughts as much an antithesis as were their looks: dark, husky man with light thoughts; blond, lean man with dark thoughts.

Not long after, Ariel and Jordan lay naked, staring

at the ceiling from twin beds in their shared motel room.

"Well?" Jordan rolled to his side and propped his head up on his hand. "Proceed."

Ariel recounted his experience with the fish, the dolphins, and the shark. Silently, in his head, he recounted the rest of it, the thoughts he'd had, the memories and emotions he'd explored while beneath the water and later in decompression.

"Something's missing, Ariel. You told me you were terrified. Damn! I would be too, but you came out of decompression looking as if you'd just seen heaven and hell stirred up in the same stew. Out with it. We aren't good friends for nothing."

Ariel looked across the room at Jordan and found his friend looking back at him. Ariel grinned. "Did I ever tell you that—"

"You love me?" Jordan cut in.

"No. That you're a pest?"

Jordan's humor played devil in his eyes. "Yeah, you did. You knocked me flat on my ass once. Remember?"

"You deserved it," Ariel said.

"No doubt." Jordan's eyes narrowed. "But you gave no warning. The first thing I thought of while lying in the grass looking up at you was that you were just like the great white shark. I'm told they give off no signals before they attack. No circling, no posturing, no nothing. They just move in and attack."

Ariel stared at Jordan, but he wasn't seeing his friend. He was seeing a burly dockworker. "You've got to expect requital when you've begged for it."

Jordan observed Ariel's tight jaw and distant look. "You aren't talking about me, are you?"

Ariel refocused on Jordan. "No, I'm not. You didn't

beg for it, you only asked for it politely. I accommodated your request."

"Who *are* you talking about?"

Ariel was silent for a time. He needed to talk, but he wasn't in the habit of reciting his love life with even his closest friend. Still, the hurt he felt inside needed to come out. "If I tell you what's been eating at me, will you promise not to ask any questions?"

"Why?"

"Because I can only tell you as much as my conscience will let me."

Jordan repositioned himself comfortably on his belly. "I'm all ears and no mouth."

"That'll be the day."

He told all of it, though only indicating that he'd made love to Karen. That part of the story and his use of fantasy wasn't anyone's business, just his and Karen's. Then he came to the beginning of the past week when he'd met up with the dockworker who had put Manny in the hospital.

"It wasn't until I was in that god-awful decompression chamber that I realized what had made me goad that gorilla into a fight. Yeah, I like Manny, and if I'd been with him at the time he got that fist in his eye, I'm sure I would have helped him defend himself. But this was a week and a half later." Ariel rolled to his side to face Jordan. "I don't think a change in circumstances would have kept me out of a fight. I was ready to fight anyone for any reason at all."

"Whatever you may think right now," Jordan said, "that guy had it coming to him."

"You're right," Ariel said. "Guys like that purposely pick on people smaller and weaker than them. You know, there isn't a word quite descriptive enough for

that sort of— On second thought"—he grinned—
"there's this Yiddish word . . ."

"Right," Jordan replied. "I know the word, but it
insults the favorite part of my anatomy."

Ariel laughed as he watched Jordan jerk his thumb
down toward that favorite part.

"Anyway, by all rights, I should have gotten the very
devil beaten out of me. That dockworker was all of me
and half of you, too. But there was this weird terror
inside of me—like I had to fight or die."

Jordan raised his head and leaned on one elbow.
"You know what?"

"What?"

"I almost did that to you last Friday night when I
found you in the MBL library." Jordan let his head drop
back down onto the pillow. "You were acting like a kid
going through the terrible twos and there I was going
through my own sort of terror over your cousin. Thank
God my sense of humor still had a thread to hang on to.
Anyway, Karen helped me out of it all. Making an
unseemly ruckus in the MBL wouldn't have solved a
thing."

"Crazy situation, isn't it?" Ariel was silent for a
moment. "You and I go barging around like a couple of
fools while the ladies just walk straight on down the
line recognizing their emotions for exactly what they
are."

Jordan smiled at the ceiling. "Ladies are pretty
neat."

"You might say that." Ariel then told what remained
of the story. Again, he left out the method of his and
Karen's lovemaking. He skipped to the part where they
had been lying in bed afterward when Karen had let
him know how she felt about him. Without telling it
out loud, he thought of how Karen had said she loved

him while he was still inside of her. At the time, he hadn't noticed it. People said that sort of thing in the heat of passion.

"It scared me, Jordan."

Jordan gave him a look of disgust. "You mean to tell me that you could go through the closest shave of your life, you could look into the literal jaws of death, and now lie here in all your naked glory and say a *woman* scared you?"

Ariel grinned at Jordan and then made an unkind gesture. "Your lack of intelligence is surpassed only by your insuperable insensitivity."

"And in my more mundane language, your lack of horse sense is about to knock you on your brilliant ass unless you pack up your gear and get your aforementioned brilliant ass back up to the Cape."

Ariel started to get up, but Jordan was quicker, leaping off the bed to virtually sit on his best friend's chest. "You are going nowhere until you've slept. A few more hours of escapism will wipe out the rest of your moronic ideas."

Ariel's shadowed eyes glittered for a moment. "If you don't get off of me right now, I'll repeat a certain violent part of our history."

Jordan got up peacefully and stood watching as his rangy blond friend dressed, packed a zippered canvas bag, and walked to the door before turning around. "Jordan . . ." Ariel lifted his hand and then let it drop in disgust. "Oh, hell."

Jordan didn't take his eyes off the door as it closed behind Ariel. He knew what his friend had wanted to say. But how does one man say to another, "I love you"?

The girls playing hopscotch were gone from the sidewalk when Karen hurried away from Nicole's building. She wanted to reach the apartment in time to pack, write a short note, and drive away before Susan returned. She knew that only cowards wrote such notes, but she was afraid that if she waited to speak directly to Susan, some of Nicole's information might slip out. It was not information a man normally entrusted to his "sister."

Karen kept up a brisk pace, unaware of how last night's storm had washed the city streets, how the sky stretched clean and blue overhead. She allowed only an edge of her mind to keep her moving in the direction of Beacon Street. All other thought was given over to the past two hours.

Nicole had said nothing earth-shattering. Karen even wondered why she hadn't figured it all out for herself.

"Ariel," Nicole had said as if thinking aloud, "must have been an extremely sensitive child. He's certainly an extraordinarily sensitive man." She placed the tip of her finger on her cheek in an unconsciously pretty gesture. "I believe his father's almost constant absence felt to Ariel as if his father didn't want him."

Nicole explored the father-son relationship for Karen with an attitude of only just now having realized the truth, but Karen sensed that this woman had spent great blocks of time considering it.

Nicole left the subject of Ariel's father and moved on to his mother. "Perhaps, in a small boy's mind, a mother who dies senselessly doesn't love her son enough to stay around."

And an hour later: "He took his father's death harder than his mother's."

"What makes you say that?" Karen had asked.

"Because Ariel came to see me the day of the funeral.

As filled as he was with grief, his stronger emotion was anger. He and his father had finally come together, and when he retired from the merchant marine, Joshua Singer planned on joining his son in business. Ariel was to do all the work of the marine biologist while his father would pilot the boat they wanted to buy. His father would also maintain the equipment, attend to the books, and do whatever else cropped up on the periphery of marine consultation.

"But the plans and the hope within him died right along with Joshua. Once again, Ariel had been abandoned by someone he loved. And so, he stood in this living room the day of his father's funeral and vowed he'd never allow the smallest part of his history to be repeated again."

Nicole sighed. "I tried to make him see that such a promise meant he'd never know love again, but he wanted me to tell him what good love could do him. What could I say? You don't understand love's goodness without experiencing it. His last words are particularly important to you, Karen."

Karen raised her brows but said nothing. She had the feeling she wasn't going to like what came next.

"He said his work entailed travel and that he loved what he did too much to ever give it up for a woman. He said he was just like his father, only smarter. He wasn't going to fall in love, get married, and have children who would forever remain fatherless."

Nicole paused, leaned back in the couch, and gazed intently at Karen. "I think he loves you and it's scared him right out of his wits. I've never known Ariel to run from anything in his life. He's not a coward. But, because of this, I think there's still hope for the two of you."

Karen couldn't remember any of the long walk she'd

just taken. She came back to the immediate present only after closing the apartment door behind her. But her mind wandered again as she packed up her few belongings and then went to the kitchen to find a slip of paper.

She hadn't been able to contain the question. "Nicole, you don't seem like . . . I mean, you're so intelligent and understanding and . . ."

Nicole laughed. "If it eases your mind any, I'm no longer in that particular business—if I ever was. Actually, I was just terribly obsessed with making my doctoral dissertation in psychology as authentic as humanly possible."

Karen's jaw dropped but not even the tiniest peep escaped.

"Originally, I planned to write on the prostitute's place in society. After meeting Ariel, however, I changed my mind. My dissertation ended up being on something I felt was more important. It was on the long-range effects of parental death." Nicole paused, her eyes sparkling mischievously. "I've been teaching night classes ever since."

Karen had to laugh. Nicole wasn't just a professor, she was a mind reader too. She'd picked up on Karen's notion of the reason for sleeping so late in the day.

"Nicole, did you ever tell Ariel the truth?"

"No, and because I felt guilty lying to him, I tried to help him with his problems even as I used him for my own purposes." Nicole twisted her hands in her lap, watching them for a moment. "Ariel has haunted me for years. I think, if the love you two have for each other wins out, somehow I'll be vindicated."

Karen gave up trying to find a clean piece of paper and, instead, scribbled her note on a small brown paper bag. It was brief and truthful, but not at all revealing.

She wrote that she *had* been bothered by something, that a long walk had cleared her head, that a solution had occurred to her, and that she was heading immediately back to Falmouth to act on her decision. She'd call as soon as she could.

Before leaving, Karen called the airport for flight times and connections to San Salvador. She wasn't disappointed by having to wait until the next day. It would give her time to pack and to plan what she'd say to Ariel when she found him.

Ariel gazed out the plane window as he fastened his seat belt for the landing. The water in the bay glistened in the late-summer sun, but he didn't really see it, he was looking inside himself.

The offer had stood for several years now. He'd never accepted the job at the institution because he wasn't sure he wanted to stay on the Cape and make such a permanent commitment. He was sure now. Sure, that was, if Karen would have him.

The plane was descending quickly over Boston, the city where he'd built years of memories. I ought to go see Nicole one of these days, he thought. I wonder what she's been up to since I saw her last time? Hell, it's been years. She probably wouldn't even remember me. Funny. She never seemed the type to go into that line of work.

Chapter Nine

By six-thirty in the evening, Karen was sitting at her kitchen table wondering what to do next. She was packed, she'd made dinner—not that she'd eaten any of it—and now, unless she found something to keep her busy, she knew she was going to start finding very strong reasons for not going ahead with her plans. She scraped back the chair, picked up her full dinner plate, and brought it over to the sink.

How could she say to Ariel that she'd never die and leave him? It was a foolish statement and she was sure Ariel would think so too. Besides, what if Nicole was all off base? What if the truth of it was simply that Ariel didn't love her? But if he didn't love her, then why had it felt as if he did? Karen shook her head. This was ridiculous, she scolded herself, start over again.

Okay, what if she told him that she loved him enough to give up her practice and follow him just the way Susan was going to follow Jordan? No good. She knew that it would be all right for a while, but she might end up blaming Ariel for her lost career.

Karen's resolve was ebbing away. She stared at the cold food stuck to the dish in the sink and then turned her back on it. She had to get out of the house. Get some fresh air. Take a drive. Something.

She snapped and zipped her jeans and then stood in

front of the mirror staring at her naked breasts as she
hooked her bra. She began slipping the straps over her
arms when, suddenly, she pulled them back off,
unhooked the bra, and threw it onto her bed. Aloud, she
said, "What difference does it make? You feel naked
inside . . . you might as well be half-naked on the outside.

When she pulled the peasant blouse over her head
and the soft material fluttered down onto her breasts,
she sighed at the sensation and the memories that the
blouse evoked.

She'd been wearing this same blouse when Ariel had
taken her to his cottage for swimming in the ocean, for
eating corn and lobster, for making love in the jungle of
an Amazon's mind.

Karen ran down the stairs, slammed the front door
behind her, and drove away from the house and her
memories. She didn't see the deceptively sedate white
BMW pull up in front of her house; she was already a
block away.

She drove in a light trance, her body responding
automatically to the curves in the road, to the cars in
front of her. Her mind was turned in another direction,
however, pulling her inexorably to a place where there
was a beach and beautiful visions of the past.

The cottage was dark, as she knew it would be. She
turned off the headlights and the engine and then sat
very still, wondering how she'd come to be here, of all
places. Was this the beach she'd meant to come to? Yes,
she realized, she could converse with the ghosts of two
people here.

She stepped out of the car, glad for the nearly full
moon in the clear sky as she carefully went down the
short but steep hill leading to the beach. When she was
halfway between the hill and the water, she took off her

sandals, dropped them next to her, and just stood there with the sand seeping up between her bare toes and the stiff ocean breeze cooling her face.

The foamy shore was illuminated for a moment, startling Karen. She spun around to locate the light's source, but she saw only the dark, indistinct outline of the cottage. It must have been a passing car.

She turned back to face the ocean. Wait a minute, she thought, this is a dead end. The road's private.

She turned toward the hill once again and saw him; Ariel coming down the hill, Ariel walking through the sand, Ariel standing tall and blond and ethereal on the moonlit beach close to her, staring into her eyes, saying nothing.

Karen's heart pounded so hard that it hurt. She couldn't have spoken had she wanted to, but she couldn't look away from him either. She ran her eyes over and under all the masculine angles of his face, over the high cheekbones, the strong brow, into his large eyes. Then, she was hearing the soft, deeply resonating tones of his voice.

"Karen, I want to start over again . . . not back to the beginning, but just to that place in time when you told me you loved me."

"Oh, my God, Ariel, what do you *want* from me?"

Ariel gently wiped away a tear from her face with his fingertips. "I want your love."

"You have that." Her voice was barely audible over the sound of long, low waves brushing at the shore.

"Even though you know I was a coward?"

She saw pain in his eyes and the pain was hers, too. "No, Ariel, not a coward. A man so gentle inside that he feared the consequences of being loved. But you don't have to worry. You don't have to marry me. You don't have to even love me back because—"

"Stop. I have something to tell you, a whole lot to tell you. Come back with me to the cottage, where I don't have to shout above the ocean."

Karen went with him, her mind filled with fears. Would he do it to her all over again? Would he take her away on a fantasy trip? She shouted silently to herself that she didn't care. A fantasy was better than nothing at all.

Ariel switched on the light and closed the door. Karen vaguely noticed the canvas bag and miscellaneous items that might be parts of diving equipment lying just inside the door, as if they'd been dropped there and then forgotten.

Ariel took her cold hand in his. "Karen, I've just been to hell and back again. And while I was in hell, I found out something." He dropped down into one of the green beanbag chairs and pulled Karen down into it with him. "I have a story to tell you and I'd like to hold on to you while I tell it. It terrifies me just to think about it."

Slowly, trying to leave out no detail, trying to make Karen understand all that had happened to him while he was in the Bahamas, Ariel talked. When he told her about the school of fish, the dolphins, and then the shark, Karen's hands began to shake. When Ariel took her trembling hands in his, she found that he too was shaking.

He told her about the time spent in decompression and his thoughts while he was there. He told it all except for the part where he'd cried—that was only for him to know.

He finished the story by repeating Jordan's words. "He said that my lack of horse sense was about to knock me on my brilliant ass unless I packed up and got my aforementioned brilliant ass back up to the Cape." Ariel grinned at her. "Do you love my brilliant ass too?"

Karen laughed. "Yes, I love your brilliant face, your brilliant arms, your brilliant legs, and even your brilliant ass."

He tilted his head to the side and whispered, "Would you like me to touch every part of *you* that *I* love?"

"How many parts are there?"

Ariel put his lips to her ear and spoke softly. " 'How do I love thee? Let me count the ways . . .' "

One by one, Ariel removed the pins from Karen's hair until it slid down into a thick, darkly gleaming cascade. Squeezing it into his palm, he closed his eyes and buried his face in the delicately scented waves. "Soft and sweet like rose petals on satin . . . that's one."

Moving her hair aside, he ran his tongue around behind her ear and down the nape of her neck. "Tangy. Lemonade on a hot summer's day. That's two."

"Ariel?"

"Woman, you're interrupting my mathematics."

"But, Ariel, aren't you going to, um . . ."

"Marry you? Yes, when I get done counting."

"No, that's not what I was going to say." She blushed violently but couldn't bring herself to voice her thoughts.

"Karen, in the words of a most renowned celebrity . . ." He paused to nibble along her finger as if it were a carrot. "What's up, doc?"

"Aren't you going to create a fantasy?" There. She'd said it.

Ariel's eyes smiled at her, but he said nothing until he'd reached up under her blouse, pulled it up over her head, tossed it away, and bent his golden head to bring her nipples into firm little peaks with the warmth of his mouth and tongue. "Gumdrops from which to suck the sweetness. That's three."

And he continued his count as he pulled her to her

feet, undid her jeans, and watched as she stepped out of them, her panties having gone the way of the blue denim. His eyes inched down her entire length and back up again as he removed his own shirt and jeans. He moved his body up to hers and pressed her to him, his hands on her buttocks, pulling her closer still. "Pillows to nestle into on a lazy Sunday afternoon. That's four."

Now Karen realized why he hadn't answered her question about fantasy. She took his hand and led him into his bedroom. Turning on the overhead light, she said, "I want to count too, but I want to see each number clearly."

They lay down on the bed, skin on skin, and Karen said, "Let me catch up to you." She touched her lips to his, running the tip of her tongue from corner to corner. "A place of music singing love to me all night long, Ariel's song. That's one."

Together, they counted the ways in which they loved. They were close to fifty by the time they'd explored and touched and caressed every place on each other's bodies. Their breath came fast and was spiked with intermittent moans of longing when Ariel rose to his knees and drew Karen up until she was suspended just a fraction of an inch above him. She looked into his eyes and he looked back into hers.

As she eased herself down onto him, she watched his eyes, watched what her envelopment of him did to those eyes, and she saw herself reflected in them. She knew that she'd never again be able to see herself in any other way. His eyes were a mirror for a fantasy, a fantasy come true of Karen and Ariel.

Ariel's voice sounded like the wind in dry summer grasses. "This feels like forever."

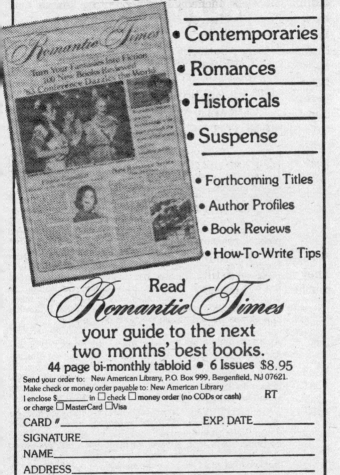

RAPTURE ROMANCE

**Provocative and sensual,
passionate and tender—
the magic and mystery of love
in all its many guises**

NEW TITLES AVAILABLE NOW

(0451)

#97 ☐ **LOVE AND LILACS by Kathryn Kent.** Gourmet chef aboard an exclusive private yacht, McLain Rutherford was thinking only of business—and not of confident First Mate Coby Hunter. Yet the soft ocean breeze and Coby's moonlight kisses proved irresistible. But then McLain found out that Coby was an ambitious restauratéur and she had to decide if he really loved her, or if he was just trying to use her—and her recipes—to make his own business a success . . . . (130111—$2.25)*

#98 ☐ **PASSION'S HUE by Anna McClure.** Art journalist Daria Barrow was determined to get an exclusive interview with prickly artist Michael Kramer. But the aloof painter was tender, too, she discovered when she became his model—then his lover in an exciting, sensual affair. Yet Michael's "love them, paint them, leave them" reputation worried Daria. When her portrait was finished, would their love be over, too . . . ?
(130138—$2.25)*

#99 ☐ **ARIEL'S SONG by Barbara Blacktree.** Karen Watts was swept away by sensual Ariel Singer's sweet, searing kisses—and by a deep desire that only his exquisite lovemaking could satisfy. Yet for Ariel, love was a game, lovely fun but never played for long . . . and for Karen, anything less than forever would never be enough . . . . (130146—$2.25)*

#100 ☐ **WOLFE'S PREY by JoAnn Robb.** At last, a romance from *his* point of view! Pursuing an art smuggler, undercover agent Jason Wolfe wasn't prepared for beautiful gallery owner Dana McBride. Warm, kind, sensual, she made him realize everything he'd been missing in life. Jason would've given anything to let her know how he felt . . . but he knew she'd only be hurt more when she discovered who he really was. This time Wolfe was caught in his own trap—and he wasn't even sure if he wanted to get free . . . . (130154—$2.25)*

*Price is $2.75 in Canada
To order, please use the convenient coupon on last page.

RAPTURE ROMANCE

**Provocative and sensual,
passionate and tender—
the magic and mystery of love
in all its many guises**

COMING NEXT MONTH

ROMAN CANDLES by Ellie Winslow. Ricardo Franco, Italy's hottest rock star, wanted record executive Annie Rawlins. And though painful memories warned her to beware of a man surrounded by glitter, it was too late. As the dazzling fireworks of his kisses lit up her life, Annie watched herself being swept into the blaze of a too-fantastic-to-be-true love . . . .

A FASHIONABLE AFFAIR by Joan Wolf. When supermodel Patsy Clark found herself involved with a crooked investment syndicate, she turned to childhood friend Michael Melville. A former federal agent, he was just the man to protect her—and the lover who made her forget all past romances. But after this case was closed, would he still want Patsy—or would she just be his old pal "Red" again . . . ?

BEFORE IT'S TOO LATE by Nina Coombs. Champion bullrider Garth Kincannon was the ideal subject for anthropologist Liz Landry's study of rodeo cowboys. And though he was infuriatingly chauvenistic, a night of wild passion showed Garth could be a sensitive lover, too. But a cowboy's life was built around "going down the road." Could Garth change his rambling ways—or was Liz riding for the hardest fall of her life . . . ?

REACH FOR THE SKY by Kaser Adams. *At last! A romance from his point of view.* Unpredictable Kitty Larkin promised just the kind of turbulence flight instructor Brenden Morgan tried to avoid. But her fiery beauty was too powerful, and after a soaring night of passion, he wanted to bring their romance down to earth—even though he knew it'd be the toughest landing he'd ever make . . . .

RAPTURE ROMANCE

Provocative and sensual,
passionate and tender—
the magic and mystery of love
in all its many guises

Titles of Special Interest from
RAPTURE ROMANCE

*Price is $2.25 in Canada
To order, use the convenient coupon on the next page.

RAPTURE ROMANCE

*Provocative and sensual,
passionate and tender—
the magic and mystery of love
in all its many guises*

RAPTURE ROMANCE

*Provocative and sensual,
passionate and tender—
the magic and mystery of love
in all its many guises*

Buy them at your local

bookstore or use coupon

on next page for ordering.

RAPTURE ROMANCE

Provocative and sensual,
passionate and tender—
the magic and mystery of love
in all its many guises

RAPTURE ROMANCE

Provocative and sensual,
passionate and tender—
the magic and mystery of love
in all its many guises

Buy them at your local

bookstore or use coupon

on next page for ordering.